I0550315

All she'd wanted was a long weekend with an old friend—what she got was a fight for her life…

"Aren't you going to drop me off at the office?" Christy asked when she saw they were headed in the opposite direction.

"No time. We're close to the crime scene so we're going to see what they've got."

Again, a roller coaster ride through the hills, this time with the siren echoing off the rock outcroppings. Christy could feel waves of nausea coming on with every twist of the steering wheel.

Telling Wolfe to slow down wouldn't do any good.

She took deep breaths and tried to focus on the dashboard, hoping the journey would be short. They came around the corner and nearly hit Deputy Espinoza in the middle of the road directing traffic. Four cars were already at the scene: two other patrol cars, an undercover vehicle, and an old Volkswagen bus with faded peace symbols and the portrait of the Zig-Zag man painted on the side.

Everyone was standing around one of the weird cement sculptures that dotted the area. This one was pink. The abstract piece of "art" resembled a building block with two small square holes on the bottom and one large U-shaped hole at the top. The bottom of the U was about a foot thick and flopped over it was a body.

Christy would have preferred to stay in the car, but Wolfe motioned her to get out "You're part of the team now. Act like it."

From the perimeter of the group, Christy could see the victim was a Hispanic man. So far, this was the first Hispanic she'd seen in Burlap, other than men at the prison yard. It dawned on her that this might be the missing inmate. She was wrong.

When sheriff's department office assistant Christy Bristol takes a long weekend to visit her friend, Lennie, in the Sierra Nevada foothills, it's not the vacation she anticipated. A murder has just occurred and Christy is conscripted by the homicide team to handle the reports. To add to her frustration, she gets in a fight with Lennie over her friend's arrogant boyfriend and has no place to stay. The detectives put her up in a forest ranger's cabin while he is away fighting fires.

As the body count grows, it becomes apparent the killer is targeting undesirables in the town of Burlap. One victim's girlfriends calls Christy and accuses a deputy of the murders. Christy doesn't know whether to believe the snitch or not. Could a killer really be hiding behind his badge? Using astrology, she casts a reverse horoscope to profile him, but puts her own life at risk.

And time is running out.

KUDOS for *A Snitch in Time*

In *A Snitch in Time* by **Sunny Frazier**, Christy Bristol is a police department clerk, who goes up into the mountains to spend a long weekend with her friend and former coworker, who now owns a small-town newspaper. No sooner does she get there when a murder takes place and she is shanghaied by the local cops to transcribe notes for them. Christy's only hope is that the killer will be caught soon so she can home. But the bodies keep piling up. The book is fun, clever, and intriguing. It's a fast paced, intense cozy mystery—one you'll want to read again and again. ~ *Taylor Jones, Reviewer*

A Snitch in Time by **Sunny Frazier** is a cozy mystery set in the Sierra Nevada Mountains, in a small town called Burlap. Christy Bristol goes to Burlap to visit her friend, the owner of the small town's newspaper. As soon as she gets there she and her friend learn that there has been a murder. They hurry to the scene of the crime, where Christy's friend gets sent away, and Christy gets drafted into serving as the secretary for the investigating officers, even though she is on vacation and doesn't want to be drafted. Unfortunately, she has no choice. And no place to stay since she and her friend have a falling-out over her friend's jerk of a boyfriend. So Christy is put up in a forest ranger's cabin. When people keep dying, Christy is afraid that she is going to be stuck there forever. So she decides to solve the case herself—with the help of astrology and a mysterious snitch. Frazier has a fresh and unique voice. The plot is strong, the characters charming and sympathetic. The story has plenty of surprises, and I wasn't able to figure out who the bad guy was until the end. And isn't that why we read a mystery in the first place? ~ *Regan Murphy, Reviewer*

ACKNOWLEDGEMENTS

I want to thank the men and women from the Fresno County Sheriff's Department who provide stories and characters for all my mysteries.

I also want to thank people in my life who have been there for me through some tough times: Ann and Jack Scott, Rhonda and Bill Watson, Mary Frazier, Lu Gibson, the Gilson's, the Buzzerio's, Kate and Kim Anderson and Cathy Frazier.

Randy Isogawa, thank you for some incredibly funny lines to add to the story.

I'm so sorry my friend Sue never got to read this novel. I hope her daughter Katy enjoys it for both of them.

Thanks to special groups in my life: the FSO retired women, the Lemoore Women's Club, Sisters in Crime San Joaquin, Sacramento and Central Coast Chapters. Also, the Posse and students at Mount San Antonio College.

Pat Canterbury and Melissa Mangus, thank you for raising my spirits as my kidneys failed. Dr. Khine and all the friends at the dialysis clinic, thank you for keeping me alive to write many more books.

Thank you Linnea for all the birthday lunches over the years. Karyne, for the many phone calls. Joe "Toxic" for making me laugh when I wanted to cry.

A SNITCH IN TIME

Christy Bristol Astrology
Mysteries ~ Book 3

Sunny Frazier

A Black Opal Books Publication

GENRE: COZY MYSTERY/MYSTERY-DETECTIVE/ROMANTIC EL-
EMENTS

This is a work of fiction. Names, places, characters and incidents are either the product of the author's imagination or are used fictitiously, and any resemblance to any actual persons, living or dead, businesses, organizations, events or locales is entirely coincidental. All trademarks, service marks, registered trademarks, and registered service marks are the property of their respective owners and are used herein for identification purposes only. The publisher does not have any control over or assume any responsibility for author or third-party websites or their contents.

A SNITCH IN TIME ~ Christy Bristol Mysteries ~ Book 3
Copyright © 2015 by Sunny Frazier
Cover Design by Jackson Cover Designs
All cover art copyright © 2014
All Rights Reserved
Print ISBN: 978-1-626942-24-0

First Publication: JANUARY 2015

Published by Black Opal Books **http://www.blackopalbooks.com**

DEDICATION

To Peggy Waters
my #1 fan

and

Bobby Minerva
this one's for you

CHAPTER 1

Detective Bobby Razulo stormed into the double-wide trailer, leaving a stream of obscenities in his wake. The other narcs in the unit turned to look at him, shrugged, and went back to planning which cases to work this week. They automatically tuned out the rant and histrionics. Just a start to another day of Razulo and his high drama.

Razulo slammed his fist on the cheap metal desk, a discard salvaged from the Central County warehouse. A few of the greener narcs turned abruptly in their rickety office chairs, but the older detectives calmly tapped away on their computer keyboards.

"Cool off, Razulo," ordered the sergeant from his office down the hall.

Andy Perrelli might have been in charge and hovered a foot over Razulo's wiry frame, but he knew better than to confront the detective, especially when Razulo was steaming like Mount Vesuvius.

Mumbling curses learned at his mother's breast, Razulo grabbed the telephone receiver from the cradle and punched in a number. His hand clenched and un-clenched as he listened to the ring on the other end.

"Hey, man," lolled the recorded message. "This is Lester. I'm not around right now, but that's cool. Just tell me what you need. Word out." Beep.

"Mofo!" screamed Razulo into the receiver. "I'm go-ing to kill you! I had the meet all set up and you're off screwing around. Your ass is mine, Lester. I'm going to make you pay, dickweed. That's a promise, not a warn-ing."

There was a click at the other end. "He's dead," a soft, female voice whispered.

"What?"

The anonymous female let out a little sob. "Lester's lying here on the floor with his head bashed in."

"Who the hell is this?" Razulo demanded.

"I have to go." Click.

Razulo stared at the receiver in his hand, uncompre-hending. A dead snitch meant a mountain of paperwork and several deals down the drain. Homicide detectives crawling all over the crime scene. Questions. More pa-perwork.

They would find his death threat on the answering machine.

Razulo let out a howl and banged the plastic receiver on his desk over and over as if he could kill the message by destroying the device.

"Bobby, I swear to God, I'm not calling General Services out here to replace another phone," warned Della.

The secretary made a grab, but she was too late. Razulo ripped the cord out of the wall and the phone went airborne across the crowded office. Stopped by the dart board, broken pieces of plastic went flying.

"Bull's-eye," muttered Martinez. He went back to reading the newspaper.

Razulo barreled down the hall to Perrelli's office. "Sarge, I gotta go to Burlap."

"I told you yesterday not to set up anything. We've got deals to do in Del Sol and Hurtado. No riding to the foothills today."

"I gotta go."

The sergeant stopped adding stats for the quarter's meth seizures. "You're not being a team player. The other guys have to get their deals going. Burlap can wait until next week."

"My snitch is dead."

"What the hell? Which informant are you talking about?"

"Somebody killed that asshole, Lester."

The rest of the team crowded around the sarge's doorway.

"Is that who you were threatening to kill over the phone?" asked Henderson, always ready to stir the fire.

"Shut up!" Razulo hissed.

"Has homicide been notified?" Sarge finally asked.

Razulo, subdued, looked like a nervous ferret. His body twitched, impatient to launch into action. "I don't know."

"Get up there and do damage control. If Headquarters is already at the scene, you just showed up to pick up the confidential informant for a deal. You don't know anything about any homicide. Everybody on board with that story?"

The team nodded in agreement. Staying off the radar of the brass was a common goal.

"Can I steal the answering machine?" Razulo asked.

"He never had an answering machine," replied the sergeant. "Make this situation disappear."

Razulo grabbed his piece and headed out the door. Over his shoulder, he called, "Della, order me another phone. Tell General Services there was an accident."

"I swear this is the last time I'm doing this for you, Bobby." Della stomped to her office. "General Services is starting to give me hell. Next time you're replacing your own damn phone."

But Razulo was already running to his undercover vehicle, a battered pickup. He beelined out of the drive-

way, kicking up a shower of gravel as he circled the double-wide and launched himself in the direction of Burlap.

CHAPTER 2

Christy Bristol lightly touched the steering wheel of her Saturn as she guided the car around the gentle curves embracing the foothills of Eastern Central County. Every so often the hills parted and Christy got a breathtaking view of vast orange orchards below, their leaves a vibrant forest green against tan scrub.

California was anticipating another drought. Winter snow pack was scarce this year as the Sierra Nevadas disappointed both skiers and farmers. Early April and the grass was already dried out. Reminders of past fires dotted the hills. Blackened tree trunks stood barren and forlorn, a forest of charcoal.

None of this ruined Christy's mood today. The smog of Central Valley was left behind, along with her office workload. Ahead, lupine grew in thick clumps along the road, their spires of purple petals reaching for the sky. The Stones belted out "Get off of my cloud" over the airwaves.

She was losing the signal from the oldies station. Christy glanced down to press the "seek" feature, searching for another station. Mariachi music blared, the Mexican om-pah beat pounding like a German polka on speed. Religious talk radio, an ad for a furniture close-out sale— EVERYTHING MUST GO!—and Waylon Jennings crooning about Luchenbach, Texas.

The blare of a horn made her jump. Riding her bumper was a truck, frantically signaling her to move her Saturn ass over. There wasn't much of a shoulder and a curve coming up.

"Idiot!" she swore as she inched as far as she could to the right.

The truck barreled past going twenty miles over the posted limit. The redneck behind the wheel signaled her with a hand gesture that was either a wave or the bird. Within seconds, he disappeared leaving her covered in his dust.

Not exactly the local welcome Christy expected.

The people here are quirky, Lennie had e-mailed weeks before when she sent Christy an invite to visit. Christy interpreted the description as colorful, folksy, somewhere between Mayberry and Dukes of Hazzard. If the rude driver was any indication, Burlap's habitants more closely resembled America's Most Wanted.

Christy forced herself to shrug off her irritation. The sky was still cloudless, the curves hair-pinned as the car climbed higher into the foothills, pine-scented air breezed through the open windows, and red and blue strobe lights flashed in her rear view mirror.

The wail of sirens caught up with the lights and echoed around the Saturn like a tsunami of sound.

"What the hell?" Christy glanced at the speedometer, doubled-checked to make sure her seatbelt was buckled, put on her turn signal, and eased right on the shoulderless road.

The patrol cars sped past the Saturn. Whatever laws had been broken or trouble loomed up ahead, Christy wasn't the culprit.

She waited until the dust cleared, the wail of the sirens evaporated, and her heartbeat was back to normal before pulling onto the road.

So much for a start to a quiet weekend in the country.

∾∾∾

The directions to the trailer were like Lennie: colorful, jumbled, and based on amusing landmarks. "Go right at that half-round house, past the vulture tree, take the turn where there's this weird cement thing on the side of the road, and continue until you see a rickety old store.

The *Burlap Bag* is a little ways across the street. We live there, too."

Christy spotted a geodesic house peeking out from weeds on the side of the highway. There was Ronnie's Roadhouse across the street advertising biscuits and gravy. Why Lennie ignored the restaurant for a building she couldn't even describe made no sense, except to people who knew how Lennie's thinking process worked.

The buzzard tree was harder to spot. Good thing there was nobody riding her tail because Christy was going fifteen miles per hour. She looked from side to side, wondering exactly what she was looking for. A foreboding dead tree looked out of place in the middle of a schoolyard. On the top was a large nest. She watched as a buzzard glided in, catch of the day in the scavenger's mouth. Feeding time for the chicks.

The weird cement thing was a sculpture of some sort: a pink block and a square box tilting to one side with a window cut into the box. Modern art looked out of place in the shadowy woods, yet strangely primitive at the same time.

A country store appeared over the tip of a rise. The planked walkway wound around the front and side of the building. Weathered signs advertising RC Cola and Bull Durham snuff competed with the neon of Miller beer.

To get to the trailer, Christy had to steer the Saturn down a primitive dirt drive. Potholes tested the car's shocks and an untrimmed hedge scraped the sides. She pulled in next to a silver Land Rover and cussed under her breath.

As soon as she got out of the car, she checked for scratches on the midnight blue paint job.

"Hey, you got here. I was afraid I'd get you lost and you'd wind up at Kings Canyon National Park." Lennie, dressed like a lumberjack in blue-plaid flannel, clambered down the metal steps and swept Christy up in a big bear hug. She let go and held Christy at arm's length. "Something's different about you. Did you change your hair? Lose weight? You're still not wearing makeup. What's different?"

"No glasses."

"Hell, that's right. You aren't wearing specs! Laser surgery?'

"Contacts."

Blue contacts. For once, her light blue eye color, which drew too much attention for their paleness, now looked like normal blue eyes.

"Nice to see you're not hiding behind those big ol' frames of yours. Now people can actually see your face."

Christy shrugged off the compliment. Praise on her looks still was something she had to work on. One change at a time was all she could handle.

Christy slipped out of Lennie's grasp and walked over to the passenger side of the car. She ran her hand over the doors.

Lennie followed behind. "Whatcha looking for?"

Christy straightened up. "Scratches. Don't you ever trim the hedges?"

"Well, hello to you, too."

"I'm just saying."

"I bought you the damn car. Don't you think I'd spring for a paint job?"

Sometimes Christy forgot the only reason she had wheels was due to Lennie's generosity. There were no scratches and Christy felt silly. This wasn't the reunion she envisioned with her former co-worker and roommate.

"I notice you didn't bring your vintage Jaguar up here."

Lennie patted the hood of the Land Rover. "I went with rough and classy."

Christy popped the trunk and took out her overnight bag.

"Here, let me have that." At five feet, eleven inches and sturdy, Lennie had the annoying habit of persistently being the strong one in the relationship. She grabbed the overnight bag out of Christy's grip. "What do you have in this thing? Boulders?"

Christy followed Lennie up the stairs. "You told me to bring my astrology books."

Lennie swung open the door with a grand gesture. "Me casa, your casa."

The front was a newspaper office. A counter blocked public access, but Lennie led her through a swinging door at the far end that clicked shut with a magnetic lock. As she trailed behind, Christy quickly looked over Lennie's new work environment.

Three oak desks crowded the room. One was messy with papers, a tin can holding an assortment of pens, a Rolodex, telephone, three staplers, a thesaurus, and an empty Big Gulp cup.

The second was ridiculously tidy. Papers were collected in a stacked and labeled file. A blotter sat squarely on the desktop. Notations in precise printing filled the calendar squares. A photo of a calico cat scowled out from a plastic frame, and a mug with images of sunflowers rested on a warming cup holder. The mug didn't have a stain or lipstick smear marring the inside. Inside a dime-store candy dish was a collection of herbal teas.

A computer dominated the third desk: flat screen, ergonomic keyboard, laser printer on a table next to the workstation. In the corner of the room was a large copier/FAX machine. The set up out-shone what Christy worked with at the substation.

She couldn't picture Lennie working behind any of the desks. While they were co-workers, Christy marveled at Lennie's ineptitude with anything electronic. The woman could jam the copy machine in ways not even the repairman could figure out. Hunting and pecking at 20 words a minute was Lennie's top speed when she sat down long enough to type. Her ability to erase documents accidentally was an unwelcome office skill. While with the Central County Sheriff's Department, Lennie had only two useful assets: her great telephone voice, as long as she didn't have to transfer calls or take messages, and a body that wouldn't quit. Lieutenants wanted the tall redhead as their office assistant and deputies wanted to take her for a spin in bed.

The feeling was mutual.

Christy followed Lennie through the relatively unused kitchen—empty pizza boxes and packaging for microwave meals overflowed the garbage can. Lennie's cooking prowess rivaled her office skills.

Through a narrow hallway was a small bedroom stuffed with a twin bed, a white, faux-French dresser and office supplies stacked in one corner. Lennie set the overnight bag on the bed with a thump.

"Guest room," she announced, as if Christy couldn't guess. "Bathroom across the hall. The hot water takes a while to heat, so run the shower for a few minutes. Not too long. Burlap's big about conserving water."

"We're having drought conditions in the valley, too," Christy assured her.

"Yeah, well, up here it's all about brush fires. Season's starting early this year. Plus, as owner of the newspaper, I have to be a role model."

Christy turned to the task of unpacking. She didn't want Lennie to see the smirk on her face. Lennie and role model didn't fit in the same sentence.

"Jacob and I are down the hall. There's a sunken tub with a window looking out over the mountain ridges.

Pretty cool when you're naked and soaking in a bubble bath. Room enough for two."

Too much information.

"I think I'll stick to the shower. I'm only staying a couple of days."

"Oh man, I planned for the whole week," Lennie whined. "You're gonna miss the local festival. I'm offering you a once-in-a-lifetime experience." She gave Christy a light punch on the arm, knocking her on top of the bed.

"Cut it out." Christy rubbed her arm. "I have to get back to Shamus."

"Why? Is your new roomie allergic to cats or just too lazy to change his litterbox?" Lennie took her role as the feline's godmother seriously.

"No, he's bonded with Trina. She gives Shamus baby shrimp when I'm not looking."

Lennie was clearly miffed at being replaced in the animal's affections. "You shoulda brought him here. I'll bet he'd love chasin' after squirrels."

The front door slammed.

Lennie grabbed Christy's hand and jerked her off the bed. "Come on, I want you to meet Jacob."

She bounded down the hall. Being in love made her almost unbearable to be around. Her voice went to a higher range, she giggled, wore pink—a color that clashed with her hair—became coy as a virgin and seductive as a vixen. Christy preferred Lennie the user-and-abuser, her love-'em-and-lose-'em girlfriend. Not that she would ever admit that she found bad-girl Lennie more appealing. Lennie expected her to be judgmental, a character trait embedded in their relationship. Christy sometimes wondered if they fell into these old roles simply because the territory was familiar.

At the end of the hall was a gangling man checking phone messages on the recording machine. He held up a single finger, signaling Lennie to stop and stay quiet. She obeyed like a well-trained puppy. At least she didn't pee on the carpet.

Don't be snarky Christy admonished herself. She reminded herself she was a guest and therefore must accept this new life Lennie had invented for herself.

She took stock of Mr. Wonderful. His thinning brown hair was off-set by a precisely manicured goatee partially disguising thick but unsensual lips. Eyeglasses doubled as magnifying glasses and several moles on his neck drew attention to an abnormally long Adam's apple. He wore a tweed jacket with worn patches on the elbows. Too many viewings of Goodbye, Mr. Chips? Academia gone to seed? Starving writer? Or did he subscribe to the Woodward and Bernstein Fashion Tips For Journalists?

Stop being critical. Christy gave herself a mental kick on the shins. She hid her amusement behind a wide, friendly smile.

Messages over, Jacob allowed Lennie to give him a hug. Over her shoulder, he scrutinized Christy. She briefly wondered what his assessment of Lennie's best bud would be.

Lennie gestured them to connect. "Christy, Jacob."

Jacob offered a limp handshake. His hand was clammy and nicotine-stained. He stayed mute, leaving Christy to open the dialogue. "Lennie's told me a lot about you."

"She can't shut up about you. 'Christy this, Christy that.' I'll bet she's asked you to cast my horoscope."

He was right, of course. She refused to comply for two reasons. First, once Lennie heard a bit of astrological information, she'd hammer for more details until Christy wanted to shove the Zodiac down her girlfriend's throat. Secondly, Christy couldn't fudge the facts. She didn't want to be the bearer of bad news if there was something negative in Jacob's chart. No woman wanted to hear the real download on the man she was enthralled with at the moment. Save reveals for later, when reality set in and blinders came off.

"Where are my manners?" Lennie became a flustered hostess. "You must be dry as burnt toast after that long drive up the hill."

She headed back to the kitchen, leaving the two awkwardly in each other's company.

"So, this is the newspaper." Lame, but an opening.

Jacob straightened like a rod was shoved up his spine. "Just a one-man operation, but the voice of reason for Burlap. Small papers are the backbone of America.

We preserve the Second Amendment, freedom of speech."

"The First Amendment," Christy said automatically. "The Second is the right to bear arms."

He froze. "I meant the First. Up here, carrying a gun is almost a prerequisite."

Lennie sailed in, saving everyone from embarrassment. "Here." She thrust a can of Diet Dr Pepper at Christy, a Red Bull at Jacob, and headed back to the kitchen, emerging with a bottle of Bud Lite in hand.

"So, what kind of stories do you cover?" Christy asked.

"We're a weekly, so we can't compete with TV for breaking news," Jacob said. "Not that there's much going on up here, of a serious nature, anyway. We concentrate on articles that are important to the lives of the people of Burlap: school board meetings, town council, church announcements, community events, high school sports."

"We post the school lunch menu for the week," Lennie proudly interjected. "I think that gets read more than anything else in the paper."

"Yes, well." Jacob flushed self-consciously. "That's only one service we supply."

"We get a lot of calls if we put pizza on the wrong day. Isn't that right?"

"People expect accuracy in their local paper." Jacob reached for a pile of newspapers, pulled one out, and handed the issue to Christy. "You can see what we publish."

On the front page was a child holding a trophy. *BUZZ OVER SPELLING BEE CHAMP* read the headline.

"I made up the headline," Lennie said with pride. "I'm pretty good. I try to make funny ones, give people a laugh when they open the paper."

An article announcing new Happy Hour hours at The Jerry-Rig and admonishments to pick up trash along the roadside completed the front page. On the sidebar was the lunch menu. Tuesday was pizza day. Fish Sticks Friday. What else did a person need to know to live in the foothills?

"There's an editorial page," Jacob quickly pointed out.

"Jacob writes it all," added Lennie. "He's very opinionated and likes politics."

"Hmm." Christy noticed Jacob's articles leaned to the left and wondered if his opinions collided with the locals'.

"How do you think this column on astrology you want me to write will go over with the locals?"

"Most of the folks will get a kick out of it," said Lennie.

"Not Reverend Adair," Jacob quickly added. "He's all fire and brimstone, sees the devil everywhere. I told Lennie she was going to get on his bad side with this idea for a feature."

The front door opened and a slight woman walked in. She gave a shy smile and nod to Christy before sitting down at the tidy desk and dropping a heavy hobo bag on the floor.

"This is Linda, our part-time reporter," Lennie reported.

Linda rippled her fingers in the air to indicate a wave.

"She just graduated from college. This is an internship before she applies at a larger paper," Jacob said proudly. He acted like he'd given birth to the woman or was intent on playing Henry Higgins to the budding journalist.

"I've got the minutes from the school board meeting," Linda said breathlessly. "I'll have the story finished in a few minutes." She looked warily at Christy. "There's some ruckus going on at the Lehman place. Sheriff cars everywhere. They were using yellow tape again."

"Another crime scene," Jacob said with excitement tinging his voice.

"Several patrol cars passed me on the road," Christy confirmed.

"What the hell are we standing around with our thumbs up our butts? This is still hot." Lennie grabbed her car keys and Christy's arm and headed out the door. Jacob was fast on their heels.

CHAPTER 3

A trailer squatted in a stand of pines, looking drab and out-of-place against a breathtaking background of forest green hills reaching far into the distance. Yellow crime scene tape looped around several trees, surrounding the home with festive ribbons. Six patrol cars filled the short driveway and spilled out into the road. Lennie and Christy pulled up to the end of the line of vehicles, with Jacob following seconds behind.

Deputies clad in tan and olive green shuffled around outside the perimeter. They hung in groups of two and three, watching the scene and talking in quiet voices. They shielded their eyes against the sun and tried to make out who was approaching.

"Hey guys," Lennie called out.

A few men recognized her from her days at the substation and shouted back a greeting. Christy hung back, preferring not to be noticed.

Lennie sashayed past the men, giving them a good rear view of her tight jeans. She headed straight for the top ranking deputy. She held her hand out expectantly. "Lieutenant Brandt, we meet again"

He ignored the gesture. "The news didn't take long to reach you."

Jacob ambled in next to Lennie. "Crimes are becoming a regular occurrence, Lieutenant."

The lieutenant looked at both of them, annoyed by their existence. "Get away from my crime scene."

Jacob got his pen and pad ready for a quote. "Sir, we have some questions to ask for the newspaper. Can you fill us in?"

"Hell, no. Nobody knows what the hell is going on, and if we did, you'd be the last on the list to know." The lieutenant's face reddened and his temper flared. "Now, I repeat. Get away from my crime scene."

"Where's the Public Information Officer?" demanded Lennie. She looked around at the group. "Who's doing PR for the sheriff these days?"

"Sousa," volunteered a deputy standing nearby.

Lennie gave him a saucy smile, raised an eyebrow, and said in a knowing voice, "Good. That's a man who will give me what I need."

Hoots of laughter were followed by a voice yelling, "You go, Lennie!"

"Shut up and get back to work." The lieutenant turned back to Lennie. "I know who you are and you've got no pull with me. Get back to your vehicle and wait for the press release."

Lennie, used to having her way around deputies, turned on her boot heels and stomped off to the truck. Christy got ready to climb back in the passenger side when she felt a hand on her arm.

"Aren't you pretty far from home?"

Christy knew the voice much too well. She turned around. "Hello, Wolfe."

Sergeant James Wolfe gave her the same sly grin that once made Christy cave to whatever he wanted from her. Over the past two years, she'd built up a shield against his amorous overtures. He was married now—happily or not, it wasn't any of her concern. They'd both walked away from their doomed relationship intact. But, with the size of the Central County Sheriff's Department, paths were bound to cross.

"I didn't know you transferred to Area One," probed Wolfe.

"I didn't know they unchained you from your desk job at Headquarters," Christy retorted.

"Something's different about you." He studied her face. "Where's your glasses?"

"What do you care?"

He looked closely at her irises. "You went from pale blue to normal blue. Your weird eyes were your best feature. A shame you hid them behind glasses. Lose the bangs and maybe people will finally get a look at you." His teasing didn't stop there. "Or does your DEA boyfriend want to be the only one to see your face these days?"

Before she could think of a response, Lennie hustled over to the couple. "Hey, Wolfe. Tell me what's going on inside."

"Good to see you too, Lennie." He gave her long legs in skintight jeans an appreciative stare. "Seems to me you don't work for the sheriff anymore, so I'm afraid everything is confidential these days."

"Don't play the civilian card on me," Lennie said in a sultry voice. "We go back too far."

"Excuse me." Jacob pushed his way between the women. "Has there been another murder?"

Wolfe gave him a hardened glare before looking at Lennie. "Get him out of here."

"Come on, Wolfe. We need an exclusive before *The Kearny Sun* and all the TV stations get their people up here," Lennie cajoled.

Wolfe turned and called out to the rest of the deputies, "Hey, we've got Lois Lane covering the story. Anybody seen Superman?" Guffaws rang out. Instead of being embarrassed, Lennie playfully flipped them off using both hands for a double bird.

"Power of the press," she yelled back. "Now, some-body give me somethin' to write about. Do you have any leads on who's committing all these recent crimes?"

"Be more professional," Jacob snapped.

"Back off, buddy." Wolfe shouldered him out of the way and turned his attention back to the women. "Last time I saw you two you were working as private investi-gators," he drawled. "Both of you were doing a little un-dercover work—or should I say, un-covered work."

Lennie gave him a punch in the arm. "You can forget that little sex club episode. Just wipe the mental picture out of your dirty mind."

"What sex club?"

All three looked at Jacob. When neither woman spoke, Wolfe went for the kill.

"The ladies didn't tell you about their adventures in Pornoland?" He wagged a finger at Lennie and Christy. "Naughty, naughty. Oh yeah, these two got *busted* in a raid and got hauled off to jail wearing nothing but leather, lace, and a smile. Best mug shots ever. I volunteered to do the strip search."

"Wolfe!" The lieutenant's voice thundered. "Get over here. Now!"

"Gotta run. Catch you later. Stay out of trouble." He took off at a trot to join the rest.

CHAPTER 4

I thought your connections would get us a story," Jacob snarled when they got back to the office. "Looks like you're just a joke to those detectives."

Christy waited for a tart reply. When none came, she glanced over at Lennie. Her friend's face was struggling to regain composure, the lower lip quivering. *What*? Lennie didn't cry. She didn't back down to anyone. Not the Lennie she knew.

"I'm sorry, Jacob. I should have let you handle the interviews."

"Yeah, you should have. You don't know shit about investigative reporting. I finally have a big story in this berg and the jump on the *Kearny Sun* and all the TV stations. You blew the opportunity."

"Whoa." Christy put her hand up to stop his verbal sucker punches. "I don't know you, Jacob, but you don't know what Lennie's life was like less than a year ago. She handled the deputies better than any sergeant could. She ran the substation and had the respect of everyone, from the sheriff down." Okay, that was a major exaggeration—but what did this jerk know? Let him investigate *those* facts.

Lennie's face registered surprise, then the gears shifted and Christy saw a bit of the old Lennie coming through.

Jacob sat and turned on his computer. "I didn't see any evidence of that today."

But Christy wasn't finished with her reprimand. "There's a lot you don't know about the Central County Sheriff's Department, or any law enforcement agency for that matter." Christy saw skepticism cross his smug features. She plowed on. "Once you leave the department you're a civilian. They treat you like you never existed. There's no drifting away a little at a time. The ties are cut."

Harsh fact of law enforcement life. There was a place for retirees, but if you left before you put in twenty, you were just attrition. Turnover was rapid. The most valuable office assistant one day could be swapped out for a clueless office assistant the next. Working for the county wasn't like private business. Getting fired was hard, but getting replaced was easy.

Try explaining that to a person who had never worked within the system. Christy could tell Jacob was one of those rabid reporters, seeking truth, justice, and the next byline. She'd encountered his kind trying to get through the doors of the substation, sniffing for info, and bullying her by dropping the names of her superiors. Investigation through intimidation.

"What about you," Jacob shot back. "You still work for those people. Couldn't you get them to tell you what was going on?"

"Me?" Christy barked a sharp laugh. "You have to be kidding. I'm the last person to find out what the men are doing. I handle the paperwork after the fact and answer telephones. Showing too much interest raises eyebrows and suspicion."

"If I were in your shoes, I would be sniffing through the files and listening at the door."

"If you were in my shoes, your feet would hurt and you'd be fired and prosecuted."

"Stop. Both of you. "Lennie inserted herself between her friend and her lover. She looked tired and her shoulders slumped to bring her down an inch from her five-foot-eleven height. "We didn't get first dibs at the story. Our paper doesn't even come out until Wednesday. By then the whole thing will be old news. Maybe they'll have the criminal in cuffs."

"Fat chance with those bozo detectives running things." Jacob headed out the door. "I'm going to get some background on the victim. Maybe I can play the human interest angle." He slammed the door and the next thing they heard was rubber on gravel as he peeled out.

Lennie went to the fridge and grabbed a Diet Dr Pepper and a Bud Light. "He's not always like this. We don't get a lotta big news stories around here, so he feels like he's side-lined at the hoedown."

"I'm angry at the way he makes you the scapegoat."

Lennie settled down on the couch and put her feet up on a low file cabinet/coffee table. "Yeah, well, I didn't look so good out there. I wish Wolfe would forget about the whole sex club incident. Jacob already makes fun of my short PI career."

Christy joined her on the couch. "Hey, we were pretty good sleuths. Considering."

"Considering." Lennie tapped cans with Christy. "To the way we were," she toasted.

"To the way we are." Christy took a deep sip and set the can down. "You've changed, Lennie."

"Have I?" She spoke the words with disinterest.

"You're not full of fire like you were when we worked together. You were a redheaded terror at the sub-station."

Lennie put down the can and rubbed her hands together. The temperature inside the trailer was too cold for swigging beer.

"Yeah, well, I'm trying to be more professional these days. This whole newspaper business means I have to be serious." She got up and went to the thermostat.

"Is that what Jacob tells you?"

Lennie nodded. "He's pointed out my shortcomings more than a couple of times," she wryly added.

"Oh, like he hasn't got room for improvement."

Lennie slipped off her jacket and snapped her fingers for Christy's coat. She put the garments on the coat tree and turned. "You don't like him, do you?"

"From what I've seen so far, no."

Lennie went into the kitchen and pulled out a pack of cigarettes from a drawer. She drew one out and searched through the junk for a match.

Christy followed her into the kitchen.

Lennie continued to sift through the drawer. "I gotta clean up this mess. Can't find a thing. Jacob likes order."

"When did you take up smoking?"

Lennie stopped her search. "You mean when did I start smoking again? I smoked in high school."

"You never smoked at the substation or in our apartment."

Defiantly, she put the unlit cigarette in her mouth and glared at Christy. "Couldn't afford to. I'm rich now, remember?"

"I don't even know you anymore." Christy turned and walked down the hall to the bedroom.

A few minutes later Lennie entered the room. Christy was already stuffing clothes back into her overnight case.

"Don't go. I'm just being a jerk."

Christy put down a curling iron and turned to face her friend. "What's really going on, Lennie? Why are you stuck up here in the hills with some guy you hardly know and who doesn't seem to respect you? I've never seen you like this, meek and subservient."

"Are you jealous?"

Christy was taken aback. "Why would I be jealous?"

"You're the smart one, but I'm the one who owns a newspaper."

Stunned, Christy flared. "That's the dumbest thing I've ever heard you say."

"I've said plenty of things you thought were 'dumb' before. You're saying this is dumb because I'm telling the truth."

So much for a quiet weekend in the foothills. Girlfriend reunions were overrated. Lennie had obviously moved on and so would she. Christy zipped up her travel bag, hefted the unwieldy thing, and stormed out to the front office to collect her coat.

Lennie was right on her heels. "I'm not done yet."

"Say anymore and our friendship goes out the door with me."

A cough cut through the barbs.

"Ms. Bristol?" said a deputy wavering between a blush and a smirk. "Captain Hillard would like to see you at the crime scene."

CHAPTER 5

Christy felt like a criminal being hustled off to jail. Or a truant being escorted to the principal's office—not that she'd ever been in either situation. Okay, the sex club arrest came close and she knew there was a booking photo buried somewhere in the sheriff department's unofficial files—probably in Wolfe's drawer.

Where had she screwed up this time? Showing up at a crime scene wasn't an infraction of any Policy and Procedure edict as far as she knew. Not that all the rules attached to her job were etched in her memory. Just the ones she'd broken.

"I'm coming with you," Lennie announced as she grabbed her Levi jacket and purse.

"You weren't invited," the deputy shot back over his shoulder.

"Freedom of the press," she hotly reminded him.

"Don't care." The deputy guided Christy over to his vehicle and opened the back door.

"Why don't I follow you in my car," Christy said.

"My orders are to bring you in. I'm your ride." He took her by the elbow and not-so-gently guided her to the back seat like a cheap chauffeur. Or a mob hitman.

"I'm calling 911," Lennie threatened.

"I am 911," the deputy calmly reminded her.

"I'm calling Sheriff Nolan then."

The deputy shoved Christy into the car and turned to Lennie. He pointed to his name tag.

"My name is Espinoza. Badge number 3043. Here, let me give you my card." He fished around in his breast pocket and handed her a card with the forest green department logo and a contact number. "I'm sure the sheriff will love to hear from you. Bringing your friend in was his idea. Oh, and let him know I'm following his orders to the letter."

Christy tensed up as the deputy hit the gas pedal and revved in reverse down the gravel driveway. He twisted the car onto the main road and shot down the hill. Christy grabbed onto the metal cage separating her from the front seat, glad she wasn't taking the ride in handcuffs.

"Slower," she begged.

"They want you at the scene ASAP. Just following

orders." Espinoza pressed harder on the gas and took a curve without braking.

"I'm getting carsick," Christy managed to gasp.

"Won't be the first time someone messed up the back seat." She saw him glance in the rear view mirror. Her face must have been a shade of gray he hadn't seen on any drunk en route to the tank. He slowed down.

"Why am I being picked up?"

"I just do what they tell me, lady." He stared fiercely at the road. "Are you important or something?"

"No." *I'm a substation lackey with a bad case of bile coming up if you don't let me have some air.*

"Well, Captain Hillard seems to think so. His orders. Detective Wolfe vouched for you."

Christy retched. *I—will—kill—him.*

Espinoza glanced back. Concern replaced the teasing. "Do you need some air?"

"Please."

"Hold on."

Espinoza guided the car to the dirt shoulder and pulled up the emergency brake. He climbed out of the vehicle, opened the door and helped her out. Gently this time.

"Take a few deep breaths." He kept a firm hand on her elbow, holding her steady. Now his actions were very different from the confrontational stance he put up for Lennie. Cars whizzed by, locals rubbernecking. Another drug stop?

"Feeling better?"

She nodded. "Under the circumstances. Yes."

"Come on, ride up front." He carefully guided her around the hood of the car. On the passenger side, there was a sheer drop ending in a steep canyon. A wave of vertigo hit Christy. She turned away from Espinoza, bent forward and threw up the soda she'd drunk.

Christy slipped her hand under her bangs, covered her eyes and waited for waves of nausea to pass. When she opened them, a light blue handkerchief fluttered in front of her face.

"Uh, you might need this." Espinoza managed to sound gruff and concerned at the same time.

Christy snatched the peace offering (or was it a flag of surrender?) and wiped her face. Anger replaced scared and the sour in her mouth wasn't just from being sick.

"Now would be a good time to tell me why I've got a department escort."

He nudged her toward the seat. The engine was still running. "You're still unsteady and that big drop is just three steps away. Please get in the car."

Not the type to steal a patrol car, especially from the agency she worked for, Christy complied. Espinoza climbed into the driver's seat and with relief continued on to the crime scene.

"Who is Captain Hillard and why does he want to see me?" she asked.

"He's head of homicide. Don't know why they want you."

So it was a PC 187.

He turned to look at her. "What do you do in the department?"

"I work out at the Coronita Substation."

Espinoza grunted. "You're pretty far out of your area."

"That woman back there? She used to work with me. I came up for a nice weekend visit." Christy looked over at the young deputy. "You weren't part of the planned entertainment."

"Sounds like you two were having a catfight when I walked in." He grinned.

Dimples. Kinda cute.

Christy stuck her head out the open window for air. The man was driving much slower now, taking the curves carefully. Good. She needed time to think.

Was there a rule about showing up unannounced at a homicide? There were so many rules on the books she didn't know about—a few she'd broken with consequence. Usually, Lennie was the impetus behind bad behavior. Until she met the woman, Christy's nose had been clean and her life safe, if boring. Now, even though Lennie'd left the department, she was still getting Christy into jams.

Or was James Wolfe once again yanking her chain? Seemed he couldn't resist showing up to make her life miserable since their breakup three years ago. *First, break my heart then go after my reputation.* Yeah, he could be messing with her.

Another possibility was Detective Kerwin. She hadn't seen the homicide detective at the crime scene. A few months back, while playing private eye, Lennie and she had nearly derailed a serial killer investigation he was conducting. They'd worked together but kept quiet about her involvement—try to explain a file clerk's role in the official paperwork. Better to sweep the info under the carpet where all the department dirt was kept. Kerwin got a commendation; Christy got to keep her job.

"Feeling okay?"

Christy pulled her face back inside. "Yeah, fine. Thanks for stopping."

"No problem."

They traveled the rest of the way in silence. When they rounded the last curve, chaos awaited. Espinoza slowed the vehicle and blasted his horn to make a path through the growing network of patrol cars, TV vans and gawkers.

Christy braced herself. What kind of trouble was she in *this* time?

CHAPTER 6

Christy appreciated her police escort as Deputy Espinoza took her elbow and used his own to plow through rabid reporters.

"Is this the suspect?" called out an over-eager newscaster.

A woman with on overlay of thick makeup thrust a microphone in Espinoza's face. "Have they identified the victim yet?"

"Get that thing out of my face," growled the deputy.

"I'm just doing my job," countered the woman, standing her ground.

"And I'm trying to do mine." He pushed her aside.

Christy looked back to see reporters from the smaller stations already taping, reporting their version of what was happening at the scene. Facts weren't necessary to report late-breaking news. Christy'd seen enough broadcasts to know the drill. Some green news person would stand in the dark, flashing red and blues in the distance, and intone "Shots were fired in the neighborhood behind me. At this time, there is no information as to whether anyone was injured in the gun battle, but an ambulance arrived at the scene just moments ago and left. I believe it is on the way to a hospital. Police are not saying what caused the incident, but drug activity has been reported in the area in the past five months. Back to you, John."

Even real facts were reported wrong. Despite the words, *Central County Sheriff's Department* and logo printed on every patrol vehicle, despite the men dressed in tan and olive green instead of blue, every law enforcement branch was lumped under the label "police" by the media. The police department did half the work of their county counterparts and received all the credit. The public blindly went along, voting pay increases for the wrong agency. Blaming the media, members of the sheriff's department felt justified in scorning reporters and had a need-to-know-and-we-won't-tell-you policy. Animosity between the power and the press continued with the news people wondering why the deputies were so uncooperative and the deputies angry at being labeled "policemen."

Christy wasn't led into the house but around to the side where a make-shift command post was set up. This consisted of an unmarked vehicle, a van, a county Jeep and several of the department brass. Christy didn't recognize any of the head honchos, except Under-Sheriff Parker. She only knew his face from his TV appearances. The deputies at the Coronita Substation didn't attract visitors from headquarters unless they screwed up. Part of her job was to prevent mistakes or bury them in paperwork where nobody above the rank of sergeant would notice. She even hid things from her sergeant, but only so Sergeant Traynor wouldn't realize how badly the men behaved behind his back.

All heads turned in her direction when he led her to the captain. By the way the others stood apart and the deference of her escort, Christy figured the tall, slender man in the center must be Captain Hillard.

Hillard stood about five feet, eleven inches and had a boyish face, despite silver strands shimmering in the sunlight against his black hair. Crow's feet, formed more from worry than age, were already etched around his eyes.

Although his stance was authoritative, his eyes betrayed hesitation and fear of being second-guessed. Christy sensed that her presence as the only woman in the confab made all the men nervous. A strategy, that's what she needed.

Keeping these men off-kilter until she knew why she'd been called in would work for now.

"You work in the Area 3 Substation under Sergeant

Traynor. Is that correct?" Hillard wasn't wasting time with introductions or small talk.

"Yes sir."

He didn't say anything else. He just stared at her. All the men stared at her. This was a familiar ploy. They waited to see how uncomfortable they could make her. Most office assistants in this position would fill the silence with too much information, nervous chatter, a lame attempt at a joke, or aggressively demand to know what was going on. Christy kept her face impassive and her lips compressed.

"You're probably wondering why you're here." Hillard looked to the others for reassurance. They nodded their heads, encouraging him. Christy didn't respond. She didn't allow a smile, not even a blink. Hillard was clearly unnerved.

"We need a secretary on board and accessible at all times while this investigation is being conducted. You're temporarily reassigned to homicide division." He took a step backward, prepared for a tirade in return.

Now Christy's mouth opened. Not a sound came out. She gasped, unsure of what she'd heard, unable to trust her hearing. She could feel her breathing quicken. A wave of nausea hit again, this time from nerves and possible hyperventilation. *Focus.*

"We're getting clearance right now," injected a lieutenant she vaguely recognized.

He was brusque, prepared for any backlash. Most of

the brass hated to tangle with support staff, which consisted primarily of females. Because they weren't sworn officers of the law, the secretaries and office assistants were deemed harder to discipline. They were less inclined to understand what an order was or to follow the chain of command.

Plus, women had a nasty habit of threatening harassment at the drop of a cuss word or a few pats on the ass. Christy, having grown up in a military household through her dad's work with the navy, knew exactly what she was up against. She knew her strengths and weaknesses and how far she could push their brass buttons.

She closed her mouth and stared for a few seconds at Brandt. Then, with an air of dismissal, she turned back to Hillard. A captain trumped a lieutenant.

"Has my sergeant been informed of this reassignment?" she asked.

"He will be." The captain cocked his head toward a patrol car where the brusque lieutenant was on the radio. She assumed he was talking to dispatch, relaying orders.

She acquiesced with one sharp nod. Okay. Let them think she was ready to do their bidding. Meanwhile, her mind raced through a mental Rolodex of who she could contact to go to bat for her. The list was short and one potential ally was Homicide Detective Kerwin.

The men acted like this was a done deal. They split off and went to different investigative clusters around the crime scene. From an outsider's point of view, the deputies were simply standing around wasting precious tax-payer dollars. Same as construction workers who had time to wolf whistle at the ladies. Just as Caltrans work-ers seemingly loafed while watching one man work.

Too many TV crime shows led the public to believe that all murders could be solved in an hour. Impatient newscasters wanted a wrap so they could get into Kearny and file the story in time for the six o'clock news. The reporter from the *Kearny Sun* was more tolerant since he didn't go to press until later in the evening. He had a large thermos of coffee and was ready to out-wait the rest of the news buzzards.

Left alone, still in the dark as to why she was even here, Christy decided to take the initiative and find out. Sergeant Traynor would know what was in the works. If he didn't, he'd waste no time finding out for her. She fished around in her purse and found her cell phone.

"No signal up here. We tried."

Lieutenant Brandt stood behind her. She ignored him and waited for the phone to give her permission to dial. The man was right: no bars, no signal. Apparently, the commercials didn't take Burlap into account.

"I'll take that." The lieutenant was now in front of her with his hand out, expecting compliance that came with rank.

"This isn't a county-issued phone," Christy snapped. "I'm not handing over my personal property—" She dou-ble checked his name badge. "—Lieutenant Brandt."

"That wasn't a request, missy, that was an order." His mustache nearly bristled, but she could tell by the cold twinkle in his eyes that he was enjoying the role of tormentor. He snatched the phone out of her hand.

"I'm reporting this."

"Yeah? To who?" He put the confiscated phone in his pocket. "Look around you and get with the program. You have no say in what we do with you."

"I don't even know why I'm here. Sir.*" Remember protocol and your career.* Keeping her temper under control was getting harder and harder to manage. So what if she exploded and raged at Brandt? They were probably expecting her to break down into tears or meekly do as she was told. The first would never happen. She'd fight the second option.

"You were hauled in because the investigation team is going to need someone to type reports. The plan was to bring up one of the clerks from Records to do the work. When you and your sidekick showed up nosing around this morning, you volunteered. You just didn't know it, that's all." He crossed his arms, smug to be the one to break the bad news.

Typical thinking on the department's part. Path of least resistance, or in this case, path of most convenience.

"Where's my work station? I'll need a computer and a transcription machine, someplace quiet to work."

"We've got a substation up here. There's an old computer, we'll find a transcription machine. Details.

Still working them out with the sheriff."

Her situation had just gone south, or rather, up, as in up the ladder. Nobody would go to bat for her against the Big Guy. Nolan was known to mulishly stand by his decisions even when they weren't his to begin with. His handpicked staff of cronies were adept at slipping their agendas into his mindset and convincing the boss all of the ideas were his. Brainwashing was part of the dirty laundry in office politics.

"So, what am I supposed to be doing right now?" Christy looked around at the chaotic state of affairs. Hillard barked orders, a mangy dog barked back, patrol officers hustled to put flares out on the curves to prevent rear-end collisions. Local gawkers set up camp across the road with a keg of beer, the TV crews thrust mics in the faces of locals who spun tales about the victim, without knowing whose body was even inside the house. She felt like the calm in the eye of a hurricane, but her insides were churning like a tsunami.

"You're supposed to be available and wait for orders." Brandt gave her one last smirk, did an about-face and stalked off to do something important.

Activity continued to swirl around her, the men treating her like a small island in the middle of a river. She stood her ground, unsure whether to move to the sidelines, get closer to the house, or hang out near Hillard. What she wanted to do was cross the road and melt into the crowd, perhaps grabbing a beer to fit in.

A woman with a mask covering her nose and mouth emerged from the interior of the house. Christy recognized Ann Pulido, one of the department's ID Techs. Christy walked in the direction Ann was headed hoping to intercept the woman before she reached the forensic van.

"Ann," she called out quietly.

Ann stopped and pulled the mask down. "Christy? What are you doing here?" Ann looked around at the scene as if a reasonable explanation might be found.

"I have no idea. They picked me up from the *Burlap Bag* office and hauled me over here."

Ann shook her head as if trying to dislodge the idea.

"That's weird. I hear they're stonewalling the press. What were you doing over at that rag, anyway?"

"Long story. They seem to want me here to do reports."

Ann motioned her to follow. "I have to pee. Come behind these bushes."

Christy thought that must be a code for "Let's talk in private," until Ann yelled, "Guys. I need guard duty over here." Two deputies saluted her and stood guard before a thick patch of lupine.

Christy awkwardly turned sideways as Ann pulled down her jeans and started to relieve her bladder.

"If they want you to work on-scene, you'd better find sleeping quarters. This investigation is going to be a long one."

"When you say long…"

"Weeks. Even when we get the victim ID'd, you have to understand what we're up against here."

Ann pulled out a baby wipe from her satchel and deposited the piece into a plastic sandwich baggie when she was done. As she used a generous amount of hand sanitizer, she said, "Times like this, I wish a was a man. They never have to worry about poison oak or bugs."

Christy waited politely for the sound of a zipper before turning to face Ann. "What are we up against?"

Ann led her out of the make-shift ladies room and gave a thank-you wave to her two guards. They grinned as Christy fought back a blush creeping up her neck.

"See that beer bust going on over there?" Ann said, nodding across the road. "We're gonna have to depend on them for info. They aren't the most cooperative bunch even when they're sober. They call us 'Flatlanders' and feel our rules don't apply to them. Normally, we leave them alone. We turn a blind eye to most of their infractions. Can't do that on a murder."

"So, what you're saying is?"

"What I'm saying—" Ann turned and gave Christy an up-and-down appraisal. "—is welcome to the wonderful world of Homicide."

CHAPTER 7

She had to get to a land line phone. Right now, she felt like Alice down the rabbit hole, swallowed into a world that made no sense, yet was oddly familiar.

She edged toward the perimeter, determined to make her escape without notice.

"Where ya going?"

And here was the Mad Hatter.

She whirled around. "This is all your doing, Wolfe."

A feigned look of shock and surprise. "Me? No, I'm not the killer."

"You know what I'm talking about. You volunteered me to play secretary because I'm convenient."

He grinned his irresistible grin.

"You've never been 'convenient,' Christy. You're a pain in the tuckus most of the time. And I'm authorized to say that after living with you for two years."

She remained resistant. "I'm contacting Sergeant Traynor. He'll put a stop to all this nonsense."

She turned to stalk away. Wolfe roughly grabbed her by the elbow and whirled her around.

"Who decided to walk into a crime scene uninvited? You brought the press with you to boot. How smart was that?"

"Lennie brought me. She's not 'the press.' She runs a weekly paper filled with gossip and ads."

"Don't forget obituaries. Got one right here for next week's edition."

Christy jerked out of his grasp. "You made your point. Now, go do something worthwhile."

Deputies had stopped what they were doing to watch the dust-up between the former lovers. Wolfe, his pride at risk, had to get the last word.

"Traynor can't get you out of this assignment. My recommendation went straight up the chain of command. That's how much clout you have around here. Deal with it."

One insult over the line. She went after him, hand raised to slap the smirk off his face. He caught her wrist in time.

"Assault on an officer of the law. Obstruction of justice. Are you aching to feel steel bracelets around those dainty wrists?" He dangled a set of handcuffs in her face. "I can add resisting arrest."

"Oh, what the hell now?" Hillard pushed his way through the ring of laughing deputies and confronted the combatants. "Wolfe, get out of here before I have another homicide on my hands. Ma'am, you come with me."

He'd already forgotten her name. She followed, glowering, head down and lips like a concrete dam holding back a torrent of words.

He led her back to the cluster of brass hovering around a patrol car. Lieutenant Brandt was in the driver's seat using the computer, hunt-and-pecking away on the keyboard. They really needed an office assistant if that's the best they could do.

"What's the status, Brandt?"

"Dispatch reached Sheriff Nolan. He's authorized a temporary reassignment with an indefinite ending date. Sergeant Traynor got the notification by e-mail." With a flourish, Brandt hit the "send" key.

The best strategy Christy could come up with was indifference. They wanted a reaction, primarily a hissy fit. She wasn't going to give them the satisfaction. She stood her ground, literally. Let these arrogant men figure out what to do with her next.

"Welcome to the team," Captain Hillard said tentatively.

"Thank you." She eked out a cold smile. "Where will I be living?"

Hillard looked at his officers. They hadn't thought that far ahead.

"We could bring up a small trailer," one suggested.

"Does the department have one?" Nobody knew.

"How about the SWAT van?"

"I'm not giving up my van for this girl." She recognized the man as the SWAT commander. He looked ready to take a swing at the officer who volunteered his precious vehicle.

"Why? You don't want her finding all the porn in the chemical john?" The men hooted.

"She's going to need something with toilet facilities," Hillard agreed as if the idea had just occurred to him.

"There's plenty of places," Brandt said as he waved his arm to indicate the forest behind them. "All she needs is a roll of TP."

Hillard looked embarrassed. "Can we get a port-a-potty up here?"

"On it." An officer disengaged and got on the horn to dispatch.

They acted like giving her a place to pee would cover the basics. "Sir, if this investigation takes more than a day, I'm going to need more than that."

A place with a stove. And a shower. From the puzzled look on their faces, she knew they hadn't thought that far ahead.

From the road came a blare of a car horn. "Coming

through, coming through," deputies shouted.

"What the hell now?" Hillard swore. "Did Nolan decide to join us?"

Lennie's Land Rover slowly tracked through the crowd, stopping at the yellow crime scene tape.

"What's going on?" Hillard asked Brandt. "Who's this woman?"

"That's Lennie Watkins. A former employee. She owns the local newspaper."

"Get her out of here," Hillard ordered.

Brandt strolled up to the window of the Rover. "Make a U-turn, Lennie. Like I said before, you don't have any clout in Central County anymore."

Lennie threw open the door, causing Brandt to jump out of the way.

"Don't be a jerk, Brandt. I brought coffee to the crew. You all look like you could use some about now." She went to the back of the Rover and opened the door.

Inside were two huge metal coffee makers, Styrofoam cups, fresh cream, sugar, sweetener, and even little sticks to stir with. The aroma of coffee drew all the deputies to the car, even those in the house followed the scent outside.

"You've got a regular Starbucks-on-wheels," shouted one deputy.

"Shut your mouth! This is Mt. Rainer coffee, and don't y'all forget that," Lennie said, returning fire.

Mt. Rainer brand wasn't just coffee, this was Lennie's coffee. These beans had brought her instant and un-expected wealth. She was the major stockholder in the Mt. Rainer coffee company thanks to the death of her maiden aunt and namesake, Leonida Dobbs. Along with money, a vintage Jaguar and independence from the working world, Lennie inherited the best coffee north of Colombia. Mt. Rainer was cultivated in the rain forests of Puerto Rico, the same terrain that grew coffee exclusively for the Pope.

While the deputies and support staff swarmed the Rover for a caffeine fix, Christy hung back. The scrape between them earlier still felt raw. A cup of coffee wasn't going to bandage up the damage. She saw Lennie eying her, but Christy couldn't read the look.

Seduced by the aroma, Hillard and Brandt grabbed a cup. Lennie didn't seem to be an enemy anymore. The two men conversed as the steam from the coffee cups se-ductively curled up to their faces. Brandt motioned Wolfe to join them. They glanced over at Christy and plotted between sips. Finally, Wolfe detached and came over to her.

"What—you're not drinking your girlfriend's coffee? Not your brand today?" teased Wolfe.

"What do you care?" Christy said.

"I don't." He jerked his head toward the captain and lieutenant. "They want to talk to you."

She reluctantly joined them. For about a half a mi-nute they continued to enjoy the brew while looking at her. *Intimidation isn't going to work, guys.* Christy stood, arms crossed, waiting for them to break the silence.

"This is your former roommate?" asked Hillard as he nodded toward Lennie.

"Yes, sir."

"You can stay with her while you're on assignment." The captain spoke like the decision was a done deal.

Christy refused to be so convenient. They were clueless of the spat and wouldn't care. She knew they had no authority to requisition Lennie's trailer just to keep a typist around.

"I believe that would be a conflict of interest," she pointed out. "The woman owns the local newspaper. I mean, if you want to keep the investigation confidential, isn't that like putting a chicken in a wolf's lair?"

Hillard was definitely taken aback. He looked to Brandt for confirmation. Brandt nodded.

The captain then turned to Wolfe. "Great idea, detective. Why don't you find a real solution?"

"Me, sir?" Now was Wolfe's turn to fumble the ball.

Christy stayed silent. She was intent on making everyone as uncomfortable as possible.

"There's a motel up the road," Wolfe offered.

With the county budget an on-going issue, Christy knew Hillard would have a tough time selling that idea to the sheriff.

"We could hide the expense under 'Miscellaneous Equipment.' We still have some money in the kitty.

Could give us a few days to come up with a better solution," Brandt offered.

Hillard frowned, his face heavy with indecision. "Okay. Get her a laptop and a printer. No Internet. She can start on the reports right away."

"Do I get a say in any of this?" Christy asked.

"No!" they replied in unison.

"What about my car?"

Wolfe volunteered to escort her to the motel. Someone would bring her car later. As Christy walked away with him, Lennie stopped pouring coffee long enough to call out, "Christy, where are you going?"

Christy ignored her. She didn't know where she was going and she was still angry at their blow-out. Let Lennie play investigative reporter and find out for herself.

CHAPTER 8

Calling the Franklin Inn a fleabag motel would be kind. The "Vacancy" sign stayed on perpetually, and the motel was devoid of customers with the exception of couples looking for an illicit afternoon romp. In the town of Burlap, these temporary partnerships were well-known and tolerated. Infidelity was one solution to boredom.

Other than the occasional tourist lost on the way to Sequoia National Park, The Franklin Inn hosted families visiting incarcerated relatives at the level-one inmate work facility. Very, very well-behaved prisoners from the county jail were allowed to live up in the foothills away from the town. They acted as a backup for firefighters, always short-handed during fire season. There were no fences, gates, or guards protecting the community from the inmates. On the other hand, there was no place for the inmates to escape. Surrounded by huge redwoods and thick pines, the inner-city criminals were up against Nature, a force most had never reckoned with. Breaking and entering, car theft, drug dealing—this was an existence that made sense to them. In the mountains, where there were no street signs, where even seasoned hikers found themselves lost and sometimes died, the odds were against an escapee. Better to enjoy the fresh air, do something productive for the state and look forward to conjugal visits in the trailer parked above the bunkhouse.

That—plus a bar, the general store, post office, newspaper, school, pottery shop, bakery, one restaurant, summer homes hidden in the hills, rusting trailers, and a forest ranger station—was Burlap.

"You've got to be kidding me."

Christy stood outside the motel registration and peered into the ramshackle office. The grimy plastic window had a small opening where forms, money, and credit cards were passed through. A skinny woman with a cigarette dangling from the side of her mouth looked at the deputy and Christy with a knowing eye.

"Hourly rates are $15," she announced.

"We need a room for a week, Madge," said Wolfe.

"A week?" Christy looked at him in disbelief.

"Maybe longer." Wolfe slid a requisition slip under the window. "Billed to the county."

Madge snatched the paperwork. "The county still owes me for last time."

"We're good for it."

She humphed. "I read the papers. Sheriff Nolan ain't got money for jack-squat. The whole state's gone to hell." She pushed a key back through the opening. "Room 22. I don't want to hear no complaining about luxuries. You get what you get."

Please, God, all I'm asking for are clean sheets, Christy prayed as she did a death row walk behind Wolfe. He unlocked the door and with a sweep of his arm graciously invited her into her temporary home.

The room met her low expectations. A dim bulb gave an orange cast to the room. The color scheme continued with a brown and orange theme, from the bedspread to the shag carpet. A standard motel reproduction of a sailboat against a citrus sunset completed the decor.

Christy let her overnight bag thump to the floor. She pulled off the bedspread and glared at the sheets. What she wanted was one of those ultraviolet lights to see the stains like they used in the TV show, CSI. On second thought, maybe not. She shuddered to think what might glow.

"I can't do this."

"You don't have a choice." Wolfe glided a finger across the desk and examined the tip for dust.

Christy spotted a telephone on the nightstand. At least she had a land line and could contact her sergeant, her roommate, her parents and even the sheriff if necessary. She would put up such a fuss they'd be happy to get her out of the foothills.

What she didn't spot was one tiny bit of entertainment. "No TV?"

"You'll be kept too busy. Plus, reception is lousy up here. They don't have cable." Wolfe smirked as if he'd planned ahead for her discomfort. "There's an ice machine around the corner and a soda machine. Only two flavors: Coke and Diet Coke."

"Just kill me now."

"There's no refrigerator, but I've been instructed to go to the store and pick up some food. Potato chips, cookies, bread, peanut butter, whatever you need that doesn't have to be refrigerated. The county will pay for it."

"How generous of them. Junk food is exactly what I need to survive in the wilderness." Christy pulled out a chair and plunked down to sulk.

"Look, you can whine all you want, but you've been given an opportunity here. You're part of a task force and have a chance to be more productive than just sitting around a substation doing filing. Some office assistants would do anything for a spot on the homicide team." Wolfe folded his arms, body language that indicated his position was intractable.

"Then call headquarters and find that lucky woman. I'll step down in a heartbeat."

They glared at each other. "Think of the overtime," he snapped.

"I don't want the money. I want my life back."

"Then look at this as a way to prove yourself to the department, maybe even go up a rung on the ladder."

"That only works for sworn officers. I can work my tush off and I'll be forgotten as soon as you guys catch the killer. That's the reality for an office assistant." She paused. "You know what I don't get? Why are you people going all out for a single victim? We have plenty of homicides. With the budget cuts, how can the sheriff afford or even approve a task force for this one?"

Wolfe looked at her. "Don't you read the papers? This isn't the first person killed up here in the last two months. This is the third: one homicide, one labeled a 'suspicious' death. Burlap has about less than 500 people living here, counting the ones who come up to their cabins in the summer. Three deaths is a major dent in the local population. The department is pulling out all the stops."

Christy only read the weekly Coronita paper, basically a supermarket flyer. She seldom turned on the evening news. There were more than enough depressing elements to focus on at her job. She couldn't remember any watercooler gossip about murders in the foothills, but then, it wasn't the section of the county her substation patrolled.

"That's why you've been drafted. They needed someone who could type reports, handle phone calls, and write search warrants. Like it or not, you fit the bill. You were at the wrong place at the right time." He gave a goading laugh. "Get busy and make a list of what you want from the store. I've got better things to do than run errands."

If there's a bible in the drawer, I'm going to hurl it at him. She opened the drawer and found a flimsy phone book and a menu for the restaurant. Neither would crack his skull. Knowing Wolfe, he'd probably file an assault on a peace officer charge. Instead, she took a piece of paper from her purse and reluctantly started writing. The list did not include junk food.

When Wolfe grabbed the paper and closed the door behind him, Christy let the phone book fly. The "thunk" released some of her fury. She hoped Wolfe heard the warning and relayed the message to his superiors that she was *not* a happy camper.

CHAPTER 9

The telephone was the only weapon at hand. Christy dialed her apartment. Roommate Trina Garcia picked it up on the second ring.

"How's the vacation?" she answered without a hello. Caller I.D.

"Rotten. You can't believe what's going on up here."

Big sigh. "You've only been gone half a day. How much trouble can you stir up, girlfriend?"

"Check out the local news tonight and you'll see. There's been a murder."

"Ow. Who got on your wrong side this time?" Trina tsked her tongue. "You're supposed to play nice. No more murders. So, when are you coming home?"

"That's the problem." Christy let out a heavy sigh for

impact. "They're keeping me up here to do the paper-work."

"You gotta be kidding me."

"I wish. They decided to make me their secretary. And that's not the worst of the situation."

"What could get worse than working for homicide?" Trina asked.

"I had a fight with Lennie so I can't stay with her. Not that Captain Hillard would let me—they consider Lennie the enemy because she runs the newspaper. In the meantime, I'm stuck in a flea-bag motel until somebody figures out what's going on."

"Back up," Trina commanded. "What did you and Lennie butt heads over?"

Trust Trina to want to hear the personal story before the professional problem.

"This new boyfriend she's got is a real piece of work. He's all intellectual and full of himself, doesn't know anything about how to deal with law enforcement. You should have seen him plowing his way into the crime scene. I thought Wolfe was going to knock some sense into him before the brass intervened."

"Wolfe's up there with you? Interesting."

"He's the one who volunteered my services."

"That man just isn't going to let you go, is he?" Christy could hear her sly intonation.

"He's my cross to bear," Christy agreed. "Listen, I need you to pull some of your strings for me."

"Shoot."

A plan had been forming in Christy's head all afternoon. "I don't think they really got permission from the sheriff to keep me up here. I'm being told a temporary transfer has been authorized, but I think they're lying. Any way I can confirm this without going through channels?"

"Let me find out which dispatchers are working. They know everything going. Nothing slips past them. I gotta few I can tap into."

True. If anyone could pull info from the dispatchers, Trina was the one. Her network, as Christy had learned in the short time they'd worked and roomed together, was vast and powerful. She had at least one relative working in every department in Central County. Even Christy's boyfriend, Rodrigo Murietta, turned out to be a cousin.

Comforted by the idea of turning the problem over to Trina, Christy couldn't help but ask, "How's Shamus? Does he miss me?"

"Come on, you've only been gone a couple of hours."

"Put him on the phone."

"You know how stupid you sound, right? Okay, let me get him."

Christy heard a bit of a scuffle in the background.

"Shamus?" Christy cooed into the receiver. "Are you being a good boy?"

After a pause, she heard a slight meow.

"Is Trina feeding you treats?"

"Of course I'm feeding him treats. He's playing with his toys and tearing up the newspapers."

Annoyed, Christy said, "This is a private conversation. Put him back on."

"You're crazy. You know that, right?" Trina must have complied because a hiss came through the receiver.

"Shamus, I'll be home soon. Mommy has to catch a killer."

The promise sounded silly, even to Christy. What did the cat care as long he got his shrimp?

CHAPTER 10

The next day, Wolfe appeared at 7:30 in the morning to pick her up.

"Where's my car?" Christy demanded.

"We've impounded it for the time being. The captain doesn't want you to go AWOL."

"How many violations on my rights is he planning to make? I want to know so when I go to the union I'll know exactly what charges I'm filing."

"Read the Policy and Procedures manual. Everything Hillard is doing is legal. Now, get in the patrol car."

Again, Christy was transported like a prisoner to her new office.

The mountain substation, generically dubbed Area One, was a cinder block outpost designed for functionality and not much else. A gravel area was carved out of the dense brush with just enough room to host three patrol vehicles.

For normal business, the small building sufficed as a way station for deputies to use the rest room, write reports, and check in with headquarters. The facility wasn't even manned with an office assistant.

Christy was led to a cubbyhole with little privacy or room to work. A laptop was waiting for her on top of a gray metal desk. A telephone and printer sat on the right side of the computer, the transcription machine, and a stack of tapes waited on the left. At the foot of a wobbly desk chair was the pedal for controlling the speed of the transcription device.

No window to distract her, no creature comforts to speak of. Purely utilitarian. Short of a stainless steel toilet, they might as well have stuck her in a jail cell for all the amenities. This would be home for however long the murder investigation would take.

"The place looks a little bare," she remarked. An understatement if there ever was one.

"What do you want? A picture on the wall? A vase for flowers? You name it." Wolfe was enjoying himself at her expense.

"How about a coffee machine?" she shot back. "And a refrigerator for cold drinks?"

Wolfe tossed a requisition pad on the desk. "Make a list of what you need. I might be able to dig up a Mr. Coffee for you, but you'll have to make do with an ice chest. We'll get you ice every day."

Christy went through the desk drawers and found little that she could use. She quickly filled the form with an order for regulation black pens, sticky notes, paper clips, a stapler, note pads, and plastic stackable trays for incoming work and completed work.

"I'm sure I'll need more, but I can make do with this list for now." She handed the paper to Wolfe and excused herself to go to the restroom. Before Wolfe could make his getaway, she stuck her head out the door and called, "And get some hand soap! You men are pigs!"

Once she was alone, Christy looked over her space. For some reason, she'd always imagined working with homicide would be more glamorous. Back at headquarters, the homicide office assistants were always bilingual. They had to be able to translate the interview tapes in Central County, which had a heavy Hispanic population and a high number of murders. Christy never even considered putting in the paperwork to interview for a position in the department. In some misguided teenage wisdom, she'd opted to take Latin instead of Spanish in high school. While she could recognize the Latin root words on a vocabulary test, the only Spanish she knew were the few words Rodrigo had taught her. And many cuss words, of course.

Tapes were already piled up on the desk, a carpal tunnel stack full. Maybe she could get out of this temporary assignment on disability. Christy settled as comfortably as possible in the chair, which tilted drunkenly to the left. She inserted the tape labeled "Lester Lehman, Victim." In went the earbuds while the wires dangled down the side of her face and made a "Y" below her throat. Her foot found the pedal and she pressed as though giving a car the gas.

"Date: April 1, 2010. Victim: Lester Lehman, white male, five feet, ten inches, approximately 180 pounds. DOB 2-12-1979. Detective Renner, investigating officer."

Detective Renner had a nasal tone to his voice as if he suffered from a sinus infection. Christy's observation was confirmed when she heard a loud and very wet snort as he cleared his stuffy nose. All of it was caught on tape for her hearing pleasure. She released the foot pedal, closed her eyes, and leaned back in the chair.

They never learned. She'd transcribed tapes over the background noise of a busy truck stop. One time her ears were assaulted by the ding-ding-ding of a railroad signal accompanied by the whistle of a locomotive. The deputy thought it was okay to record his report while waiting for the freight train to pass. She'd set him straight by putting the earphones on his head and making him listen to the ruckus. The worst had been a burglary report at a house decorated for Halloween. The interview between the deputy and the victim was repeatedly interrupted by a motion-controlled ghoul whose maniacal screeches amused the deputy and gave her a migraine. She refused to talk civilly to the deputy for two months—thirty days for each eardrum.

Christy concentrated on the tape, cringing every time the detective wheezed, coughed, sneezed, and cleared his throat in her ears. She wasn't paid enough to sit and listen to him fight a cold. What might have been intriguing— the description of a man whose head was bashed in like an overripe cantaloupe—lost something in the distraction of the head cold. She wanted Detective Renner to take a big dose of NyQuil and go to bed. So much for the excitement of working on a homicide case.

According to the tape, an anonymous call was made to the Central County Sheriff's Department on April 1, 2010, at 0900 hours. The tipster—female—indicated that Lester Lehman, DOB 02-12-1979, was a victim of a homicide at his residence, 10223 Collier Drive, Burlap. Deputies were dispatched to the scene. Upon arrival, Lehman was discovered to have experienced blunt-force trauma to the head and was definitely dead. No weapon was found.

Detective Renner droned on through the rest of the description of the scene. At this point, Christy typed on automatic pilot. Words in her ears translated to letters on the monitor. Her brain clicked off and her hands flew across the keyboard with a mind of their own. She became one with the transcription machine. Secretary zen.

The next tape was from Detective Bobby Razulo,

Narcotics team, Case Agent for L. Lehman.

Without her consent, her interest was engaged.

Lester—she and the deceased were now on a first-name basis—was a confidential informant for Detective Razulo. He'd been busted for dealing a small quantity of methamphetamine to the detective who was posing as a fellow meth head. Returning the favor, Razulo made an offer to Lester: go undercover as a minor meth dealer—no stretch there—and set up deals with the bigger fish while wearing a wire. After five successful deals, the charges would be dropped.

Lester turned out to be a very good snitch. He led the narcotics team toward making some very big busts and contributing to the War on Drugs. He was so good, in fact, that after he worked off his contract he stuck around to play informant for money.

Christy lifted her foot off the pedal and stopped the tape. This practice was news to her. Central County, always short on cash, had drug dealers on the payroll? Interesting.

Further into the tape, she discovered the county also supplied an apartment, furniture, and taxi service to and from drug deals. His rent and electricity were paid for. Lester was living better than she was. A wave of envy passed through Christy.

Here she'd been working for $10 an hour and barely getting by when all she had to do for a free ride was to get caught sticking a needle up her arm.

But Lester didn't know when he had a good thing going. Apparently, he'd been playing fast and loose with the break he'd been given.

Suddenly, he was unreachable. The case agent, Razulo, believed his informant wasn't as invested in the arrangement as necessary. When going into a drug deal alone, the wire planted on Lester's body would suddenly go dead.

The narc team stood by, ready to rush in if the deal went south. Somehow, transmission miraculously resurrected just when the narc team was ready to bust through the door. Although Lester was searched both before and after every deal, Razulo was suspicious that Lester was back on meth and making side deals during radio silence. Unacceptable.

Christy grinned at the absurdity of what she was listening to. Trust a snitch? In what universe was that possible?

On the morning of April 1, Detective Razulo failed to reach the CI Lester Lehman via land line. Instead, he got the voice recording of Lester instructing callers to leave a message on the answering machine—equipment supplied by the county. While he was leaving a message, an anonymous female picked up the phone and informed him that Lehman was deceased. Upon arrival at the CI's current address, Razulo found the homicide team already investigating the scene. End of tape.

There were more tapes, each deputy on the scene

adding his or her version to the mix. By the end of the day, Christy rolled the tilted office chair away from the keyboard and rested her tired fingers. The thrill of the homicide investigation was gone.

CHAPTER 11

Wolfe picked her up at 4 o'clock. Instead of heading in what she assumed was the general direction of the hotel, he drove deeper into the forest and away from the remnants of civilization.

"Okay, I give up. Where are we going?"

"You'll see."

Out of patience and short on curiosity, Christy said, "I've had a long day and I'm tired. Cut out the sightseeing and please take me back to the hotel."

"You think the department has money in the budget to put you up at the Burlap Hilton? Captain Hillard has made other arrangements."

Christy bit back a snarky reply. Based on evidence

she'd heard today, the sheriff's department needed to re-think their budget priorities.

"What about my suitcase?"

Wolfe grinned. "In the trunk."

Christy took it as a sign that he'd freely gone through her personal items.

Not that his actions should have mattered. After living together for two years, there wasn't much packed away to surprise him. Wait—the bikini panties. That was one change since Rodrigo had come into her life. She shot a wry grin right back at him.

Wolfe turned off onto a dirt road. A small cabin stood in a sheltered glade. Redwoods created a canopy over the dwelling, and pine needles provided a carpet. The sides were wood, the roof tin. Wind made the redwoods sing high above but was reduced to a whisper when passing through the heavily forested ground.

The scene was idyllic, better than any summer timeshare. Being shanghaied into working with homicide was quickly turning into a working vacation.

Christy had a hard time keeping a dissatisfied look on her face. Inside, the cabin was dusty but orderly. Books were arranged on a wooden shelf above a rustic desk. A single cot in the corner was neatly made up and covered with a worn quilt. The kitchen consisted of a gas stove. A pot and a skillet sat on the burners. A few plates and two mugs were stacked in an open cupboard. A hotel version of a refrigerator sat in the corner. Logs were neatly stacked in a bin ready to burn in a potbelly stove. The cabin's only other room was a bathroom that would look small in a Winnebago, complete with a coffin-sized shower. Someone lovingly called this place home.

"Who lives here?"

Wolfe did a cursory inspection, ignoring the dust and judging the contents. "One of the forest rangers assigned up here. He's in the Los Angeles area working disaster relief. Rain is dissolving the cliffs and mud slides are burying the freeways. Serves L.A. right."

Animosity toward the City of Angels was de rigueur for folks in the San Joaquin Valley. Every summer the dry California hills became a tinderbox. Homes that survived the waves of fire were left to face the mudslides of El Nino in a wet year. While water was always needed, the soil couldn't absorb the rains and without brush entire mountainsides turned to mush. Yet, the wealthy in La La Land continued to build homes on the edges of cliffs, gambling that the view was worth the risk. This left people in the pancake-flat Central Valley scratching their heads at the stupidity of their southern neighbors. No sympathy was wasted on people with no common sense.

Wolfe went out to the car to get her overnight bag. He returned and dumped the bag on the bed.

"Okay, you're settled in. Catch you tomorrow."

"Wait!"

Christy walked over to the refrigerator and opened it. Empty. Not that it mattered since there was no electricity.

"What am I supposed to eat?"

Obviously, nobody had thought that far ahead. While the sheriff's department was very good at putting together a task force, captains and sergeants were incapable of putting together a grocery list.

Wolfe opened a cabinet. He pulled out a tin of pork and beans. "Canned food, I guess. Hobbs Market is closed. We can deal with the problem in the morning." Wolfe seemed eager to get down the mountain to his own hot meal.

"And electricity?"

Wolfe looked put out. "Okay. So you have to rough it for one night. Somebody will take care of it tomorrow."

Christy walked over to the range and turned on the burner. Nothing.

"You need propane. I'll put it on the list. Any other complaints?"

"I don't see a telephone. I want my car back. I want TV, Dr Pepper, and a hot bath. I want to sleep in my own bed. Can you take care of that tomorrow too?"

Wolfe held up his hands, palms out. "Whoa. You don't see the opportunity I've given you here. You have a chance to score points with the homicide team and maybe get out of that grimy little substation where you've been buried for years. You've been called up to the big leagues. Make the most of this murder case that's been dropped in your lap. "

Furious, Christy turned on him. "I don't want a

break. I like my boring routine at the substation. I know what to expect every day. Files to file, telephone calls to transfer, plus I get a scheduled lunch hour and two breaks. I never asked for this."

"You're a creature of habit," Wolfe said dismissively.

"Yeah, and you were the worst habit I ever had."

The line was crossed.

"I left you two years ago. Get over it. I have."

"And yet you keep showing up to make my life miserable," Christy countered.

"The sheriff's office isn't big enough to avoid you. I keep tripping over you every time I'm working a case. Case in point. If you can't accept that, why don't you go work for the police department?"

He was right and Christy was furious.

"I wish I'd never come up to visit Lennie. Now we're not on speaking terms. Because you volunteered my services for a murder investigation, I can't get down off this stupid mountain. I've made a life for myself and, as usual, you don't care. As long *you* aren't inconvenienced, you're not concerned."

Instead of taking offense, Wolfe grinned. "Here we go, bringing up the dirty laundry again. You're the one who hasn't moved on. I got married and I'm going to be a father pretty soon. What have you done except show up for work and file papers? You have no ambition and no goals. Don't blame me for your miserable life."

"I have stability. I'm in a relationship with a man I can trust. That's more than I ever had with you," she fired back.

Wolfe grinned. "Let's see how long that's gonna last."

He again turned to leave. That's when Christy noticed there was no security lock on the door.

"Hey, you can't leave me here alone without a way to protect myself. There's a killer roaming around," she protested.

"We're not going to issue you a gun, if that's what you're thinking,"

"Pepper spray. Mace. A baseball bat. Give me something." She tried to sound demanding instead of pleading. "Why didn't you deputies think about a lock on the door when you put me here?"

"Just an oversight. I'll mention it to the lieutenant." He gave her a salute and left.

Christy took stock of her new environment. She found a Coleman lantern and pulled two of the largest logs from the woodpile. She stacked them against the door. Not much of a barrier, but better than nothing.

She opened up the can of beans with a can opener that looked like it belonged on a Swiss Army Knife. Stale saltines were in the cupboard, in a Tupperware container so the bugs (or rats) couldn't get to them. The tap water was ice cold and much better than what they drank in the valley. There was no hot water for a shower so she made do with an icy sponge bath. As it grew dark, Christy heard an owl hooting from a treetop, a sound foreign to her city ears. With no other options, she finally went to bed hungry and fully clothed.

CHAPTER 12

Day three of her incarceration.

That's what the job felt like to Christy. She'd been conscripted, shanghaied, pressed into service without her consent. A stack of tapes waited for her, the pile having grown overnight.

Ice was waiting in an ice chest as promised. There was a vacuumed wrapped sandwich, bottled water, and a fruit cup chilling for her, but no Mr. Coffee. No Dr Pepper either. No caffeine to jump start her day.

The deputies were either avoiding her or had been instructed to stay out of her hair. The word must have gone out that she was less than happy with her current situation. Hell hath no fury like an office assistant scorned.

Just when the day was at its draggiest, that numb area between 2 and 3 p.m. when the body begs for a nap, the phone rang. She hoped someone with authority was on the other end to tell her a mistake had been made, she was needed at the substation. Even a call to ask if she needed anything would be appreciated. Solitary confinement was getting tiresome.

"Area 1, OA Bristol speaking."

There was silence on the other end. Christy repeated her greeting.

"Are you a detective?" a trembling female voice asked.

"No, I'm the office assistant. There are no detectives in the office right now. Can I take a message?"

Again, silence.

"Hello?" Christy asked impatiently.

"I know something."

Okay. This could either be a crank call or important information. Christy dropped her voice down to a conspiratorial tone. "What do you know?"

"I heard him threaten Lester."

"Who? The killer?"

A long silence again. This time Christy waited her out.

"Ask where the tape is."

"What tape?" Christy looked at the pile of tapes on her desk.

"The answering machine tape." The woman hung up

leaving a sharp click ringing in Christy's ear.

Christy shuffled through paperwork to locate the items entered into evidence. An answering machine was listed, an older model that used cassette tapes. Christy had owned a similar model years ago.

Whoever the caller was, she seemed to have a key piece of information. Chain of command dictated that Christy pass the info along to her superior, but who that person was in this situation was unclear. Was it Captain Hillard? She'd never jumped rank and gone over anyone's head to talk to a captain. Lieutenant Brandt? He didn't seem the type who would take her seriously. Under normal circumstances, she'd report to Sergeant Traynor, but he wasn't her confidant for the time being. She'd be damned if she'd tell Wolfe about the call, no matter if he did have rank. Brandt it was.

Just as she was about to punch in the number, Christy stopped to consider. Maybe the call was a hoax. She'd be an object of ridicule if she started asking unfounded questions. Even if the questions were valid, detectives wouldn't like being called on an oversight. Nobody liked a lowly office assistant to outshine them. It was a lose/lose situation for Christy.

She scanned the evidence list again. There was no separate mention of a cassette tape. Wouldn't someone have listened to the tape looking for clues? There were no reports on her desk mentioning what was on the tape. In fact, why hadn't she been asked to transcribe conversations off that particular tape? Homicide detectives were supposed to be more thorough than that—weren't they?

Determined to find some answers, Christy dialed the only place she could think of to handle the situation without ruffling feathers.

"Evidence," a voice answered.

"Yeah, hi. This is OA Bristol and I'm helping with the homicide up here in Burlap."

"That's the one where the snitch got offed, right? Man, the foothills have some of the weirdest cases, but this is one for the books."

Evidence must have been having a slow day. Either that or the deputy was in a chatty mood. Maybe he shared her feeling of isolation.

Christy pictured him surrounded by musty boxes full of blood-stained artifacts.

"Listen," she continued in a bored tone, "I'm looking at the evidence list submitted by Deputy Espinoza and I see an old answering machine listed. I was wondering if the recording cassette was included. I don't have a separate listing for it. It's not a big thing, but I want to be thorough. If it's not there, I don't want to be hung out to dry for not doing my job."

"Hold on, I'll check."

The phone wasn't put on hold with Muzak to entertain her. She heard the deputy's footsteps fading away, then coming back to the desk. There was a "thump" as a box was dropped next to the receiver.

"Here it is, a real piece of crap. I don't see a cassette inside. Nothing in the box either."

"Okay, the detective must have left it off the list for a reason. Maybe someone in the lab is checking it over for prints."

"No problem. Hope you guys catch the killer."

"We're sure giving it our best." Christy wished him a good day and hung up.

Interesting. Who would want the tape badly enough to snatch it from the answering machine? Obviously, the killer. The woman caller indicated there was a threatening message on the missing tape. She must have been in the house when it was recorded. Maybe she was a neighbor, a relative, or a girlfriend.

Christy could finally see a way out of working on the case. She'd simply solve it.

c/ɔc/ɔ

Before heading back to the cabin, Christy decided to make a food run at the only grocery store in town. Hobbs Market was nothing more than a general store. It carried staples like milk, eggs, butter, sugar and bread. There were sodas and beer in the refrigerator cases, pork rinds, and potato chips on the snack shelf. Cigarettes and snuff were plentiful. Fresh fruit and vegetables were not.

Christy went to the soda aisle and searched in vain for her favorite.

"Excuse me." She addressed the woman behind the counter and was greeted with a smile minus a few teeth. "Can you tell me if you carry Diet Dr Pepper?"

"Why, shure we do," the woman replied. "Got some in just yesterday."

"I don't see it on the shelves. Is it in the back?"

"Oh, so you like that soda, too." The woman scratched her head and a few flakes of dandruff dusted the counter. "Must be a popular brand for you Flatlanders."

Christy remembered being told that "Flatlander" was a term the foothill folks called anyone who lived on the valley floor. The epitaph was spit out like the insult it intended to be.

"I'd like to buy a six pack if you have one in the back."

The woman looked her up and down, then picked up a tin can and spit in it. "Nope, we're all out. Truck won't be back for a week."

What had started out to be a lousy day in a worse week was getting more bleak by the second. "Is there any place in town where I can buy a Dr Pepper?"

"You might try the newspaper office. Redhead up there bought every Dr Pepper in town, even cleaned out the soda machine at the gas station."

Lennie. Christy pressed her lips together to make a tight, thin line. She turned on her heel and stalked out of the store. The Burlap Bag trailer defied her from atop the hill.

Christy stood at the foot of the steps and yelled "Lennie!"

The front door opened and Lennie lazily came to the porch. She draped herself against the railing. "You want something?"

"You know what I want."

Lennie's hand came from behind her back. She held a can of Dr Pepper out to Christy. Seeing the droplets of condensation made Christy's mouth ache for a taste.

"I think we have something to talk about," Lennie said.

"I'm not in the mood for talking," Christy shot back.

"You don't want to discuss our friendship over a drink?" She wiggled the can back and forth like she was teasing a dog with a bone. "There's more where this came from. In fact, I've got several cases filling up the back room."

I am a weak woman. Lennie knew this tactic would work. There were many of her favorite things Christy was willing to give up: See's caramels, Starbuck's frappachinos, the Sunday funnies, movie theater popcorn. Dr Pepper was non-negotiable.

CHAPTER 13

Look," Lennie began, "I'm not apologizing for what happened."

"Don't expect me to apologize," Christy shot back.

Lennie picked up a pack of Camels, hesitated, then slipped them into a kitchen drawer.

Christy scoped out the trailer, checking to see if they were alone.

"Don't worry, Jacob's not here. He went into Kearny to try to worm something out of Sheriff Nolan. He wants to play investigative reporter so he can write a Pulzer prize-winning story about this murder."

"Pulitzer," Christy corrected.

"See, there you go again. You always have to point

out how stupid I am, even though you know what I mean."

Christy was taken aback. "I've never called you stupid."

"But that's what you think. You've read lots of books and I know you're smarter than me but you don't have to rub it in my face." Lennie's face scrunched up, holding back tears. In all their years of knowing each other and working together, Christy had never seen her be so vulnerable. "You think I'm full of myself owning a newspaper when I never bothered to read one."

"Well, your new line of work did catch me off-guard," Christy admitted. God, she sounded snarky even to herself.

"Who would have thunk it, right? Ignorant Lennie publishing a newspaper. You have no idea what I can do when I put my mind to it."

That wasn't true. Christy was constantly amazed at her friend's fortitude and ingenious ways of getting out of trouble. Of course, Lennie had interesting ways of getting both of them into trouble in the first place. Would she have dressed up in bondage wear or ever stepped foot into a sex club if Lennie hadn't forced her? There's no way she would have played detective if Lennie hadn't convinced her they could solve a case and find a missing man. Breaking every rule in procedures manual was against Christy's nature. Lennie ignored rules when it suited her.

Okay, maybe Christy was a little judgmental. Lennie's lack of morals never failed to astonish and revolt Christy. Sleeping with whichever male caught her fancy was a trait in Lennie that she couldn't condone. Maybe Lennie's Amazon height, bra size, and flaming red hair gave her a sense of entitlement. Rules of conduct didn't apply. Now, with the addition of inherited fortune, Lennie could do whatever she pleased. Not that being dirt poor ever stopped her before. The difference was that people now seemed to be more forgiving. Money made bad behavior acceptable.

"I think you've changed, that's all. I don't understand the new Lennie. I'm glad you're exploring new careers and I'm glad your fortune allows you the freedom to experiment. But, running a newspaper? You've never expressed the slightest interest in journalism. I have a hard time believing you've found your passion." Harsh, but true. Did she have the nerve to deliver the kicker? Her mouth made the decision for her. "You just want to impress this jerk Jacob. Isn't sleeping with him enough? Do you have to finance his dreams of glory? Is that what you think you need to do to impress a man? Spread your legs and give him money?"

Both women squared off, the fuse of unspoken anger lit. There was no stopping the spark racing to send their relationship up in flames.

"Take your damn Dr Pepper. Take it all." Lennie kicked a case from the corner of the kitchen. "I don't want to see another can of this shit again. And I don't want to see you again."

The door swung open and hit the wall with a bang.

"There's been another murder," Jacob announced. The glee in his voice was hard to miss.

CHAPTER 14

The second victim had been dead at least a week. Technically, that made him the first victim if the murders were connected. The house, more like a tar papered cabin, was set back in a thicket of fir trees. The Christmas tang of pine pretty much covered the smell of decay. An anonymous caller had reported the death of Fremont Hobbs, the squatter who called this shack home.

When Christy, Lennie, and Jacob arrived on the scene, yellow crime tape was already in place playing ring-around-a-rosy in the surrounding trees. Deputies stood around, not really guarding the crime scene. There was no use protecting a rotting corpse at close range. Let the detectives deal with the smell, the overflowing trash, and whatever rodents happened to consider Hobbs dinner.

Jacob was already pushing his way in and pushing the buttons of the deputies guarding the perimeter.

"I'm Press. I want to speak to someone in charge."

A look of scorn crossed the deputies' faces and a sardonic grin flashed between them. "We don't care who the hell you are," replied one. "Get away from the crime scene."

"Can I quote you on that?" Jacob had his pen poised over a reporter's notepad, as if the pen were really mightier than the sword. Or, in this case, a Glock.

"Sure, you can quote me. And here's a few more sound bites for your column."

Before a spew of obscenities followed, Lieutenant Brandt walked out of the shanty and elbowed his way between the guards.

"Didn't take long for the word to spread," he said, taunting the threesome. He focused a laser glare at Christy. "Are you back in the enemy camp?"

What was she supposed to say? "No, I was breaking up with my best friend for putting up with this jerk when your homicide inconveniently interfered." Instead, she kept her lips tightly shut.

Behind the lieutenant followed an entourage: a uniformed patrol sergeant, his trainee, who promptly vomited over the barrier of yellow tape and two men in civilian clothes. They personified "plain-clothed detectives" in the worst way with cheap sports jackets, wrinkled shirts, and thin ties from another era of fashion. It was more a matter of low wages and frugality rather than bad taste. Their pant legs were dirty from scoping out the inside of the house. Decomposition perfumed their clothes. It didn't take an astrologer to see another bill from the dry cleaners in their future.

No sirens this time. The forensic team pulled up in their van and Ann Pulido stepped out. She had a Vicks bottle in her hand and was applying the gel under her nose.

A blue face mask dangled from her arm, latex gloves already snapped on. She was ready for business.

Ann gave Christy a slight nod and ducked under the tape. A tech followed with a fingerprint kit and camera. They stopped at the door to put on booties before entering. The coroner was not far behind.

More patrol cars pulled up and parked on the narrow roadside. So far, no gawkers except for Christy, Lennie, and Jacob.

Only one person in town knew of the death, and the anonymous caller would be stupid to call attention to the fact. Even the news vultures were in the dark. Channels 30, 47, and 24 weren't listening to their scanners today. The TV late night news would miss the story and the *Kearny Sun* was already put to bed.

However, there was Jacob. The *Burlap Bag* had the exclusive.

"Lieutenant, can you confirm that the victim is Fremont Hobbs?"

"Yeah, that's Fremont." Brandt turned away to talk to one of the deputies.

"Can you definitively say when he was murdered?"

Brandt turned back and looked at Jacob as though he were a maggot feeding off the corpse. "No, I can't definitively say shit. I wasn't there when it happened. I'm not even calling it a homicide at this point. And you better not call it murder in your notes."

"Do you think there's a connection between this death and the murder of Lester Lehman?" Jacob persisted.

A mask of impassiveness came over Brandt's face. "No comment."

"Does that mean you think there is a connection, or are two bodies discovered a day apart just a coincidence in your mind?"

Too far, Christy thought. She looked at Lennie. A blush of embarrassment colored her friend's face.

"No comment means I don't have to talk to shit like you," Brandt said. "Lennie, get him out of my face before I do something that will get me busted down to sergeant." He turned on his heel and stalked away.

"I'm not done with you yet," screamed Jacob.

Lennie grabbed his scrawny shoulders and held him back from chasing after the lieutenant.

He pulled free and turned his anger on Lennie. "You

aren't much help, are you? You stand there and let your precious deputies walk all over me. Where's the power of the press? You can't run a newspaper and handle authorities with kid gloves. It's a conflict of interest."

"The only conflict I see is whether I'm going to lock you out of the bedroom tonight."

Christy was beyond embarrassment. There was no way she was going to get in the car and ride back with these two.

To her relief, the decision was made for her.

"Ma'am, the lieutenant says I'm to take you back to the cabin." The trainee took her elbow and firmly guided her away from the squabblers. Their argument didn't need her as an audience. There were more critical things for her to worry about.

CHAPTER 15

L ooks like I'm going to be up here longer than I thought." Christy cradled the phone to her ear as she talked to Trina. In the background, she could hear the sounds of the busy substation. It made her long to get back to her desk and mundane work she understood.

"What, they can't solve the murder in three days?" Trina asked sardonically.

"There's been a 'suspicious death.' Nobody's calling it a murder but that's how they're handling it."

There was silence on the other end. "Sergeant Traynor's here. You want to talk to him?"

"Of course." Traynor must be missing her by now. Maybe he could persuade the homicide division to send one of their own office assistants to do the dirty work.

"Christy, how are you handling things?" The sergeant's voice was cheery, not at all what she had hoped for.

"Not very well, I'm afraid. The detectives put me up in a rustic cabin in the woods, and I'm working in an office with a laptop and no coffee pot." Christy tried hard not to whine but couldn't stop herself.

"That doesn't sound so bad. I'll bet the foothills are beautiful this time of year. I used to go up there fishing."

Was he kidding? "I'm not on vacation. They have me transcribing tapes in a tiny room and I'm alone most of the time until they need me."

He actually laughed in her ear. "Think of the overtime you're earning."

"Sarge, you have to get me out of here."

Traynor used a fatherly tone reserved for the young women who worked for him. "Christy, I have no pull. Your assignment was authorized by Sheriff Nolan. The only thing you can do is make the best of a tough situation. Think of the experience you're getting. Besides, you have Lennie up there and I'm sure you are enjoying your time together."

She hadn't intended to let anyone know of the falling out with her best friend.

The argument would be viewed as petty and would be dismissed as a hen fight.

The women were identified as trusted friends for so

long in the department that one little fight wouldn't be taken seriously.

"I'm not talking to Lennie."

"What?" Traynor said with the first concern in his voice. "Did you and Lennie have a falling out?"

"She's got a boyfriend up here and he's being a real jerk to her. I can't stand watching her be cowed by a man like that and I told her so. Plus, she thinks she can run a newspaper when we both know that the only thing Lennie reads are tabloid magazines." Christy heard a catch in her voice and felt frustrated tears welling up.

"Sounds like someone's a little bit jealous," teased Traynor.

That was totally uncalled for. Christy chose to ignore the remark and pressed on. "They found another body yesterday. Now I'm going to be stuck up here even longer."

Apparently, Traynor hadn't heard the latest via the headquarters grapevine. "Who's the victim? Do you have a name?"

"I think his name is Fremont. I don't know if that's the last name or not."

"Fremont Hobbs. I remember him when I worked up there before I made sergeant." Traynor clucked his tongue. "I guess it was just a matter of time."

"What do you mean?"

"Fremont is one of those fellas who thinks the property belongs to him. His parents built a cabin up there, raised a swarm of kids and then couldn't pay property tax or electricity or grow food. They got evicted and the property sold, but Fremont still feels it's Hobbs property. Every now and then, we'd have to arrest him or one of his kin, but they fly right back to the homestead like carrier pigeons. Still, I hate to see him murdered."

"They don't know if he was murdered," Christy corrected. "Somebody reported the body but he'd been dead for a while before anyone found him."

"Two dead derelicts in a week is a pretty high ratio for such a small community," Traynor mused. Then his tone changed. "Well, gotta run. Good talking to you. Hope to see you soon. Here's Trina."

Miffed at his dismissal, Christy was anxious to hang up. When she heard Trina's voice she said, "Looks like I'm not missed at the office. Sounds like you're doing all right without me."

"Naw, we all miss you. Work has been slow around here, not like all the excitement where you're at." She was interrupted by hooting and hollering in the background. Several male voices called out "Trina, get over here."

"What's going on?" Christy asked.

"Oh, you know, just a birthday party for me. The guys got a cake and they want to light the candles. You know how they are when chocolate cake is around." She put her hand over the receiver and called out "Okay, I'm coming. Hold your horses." To Christy she said, "I gotta run."

"Happy birthday," Christy quickly inserted.

"Thanks. And hey, Shamus is doing okay. He misses you. I gave him your bathrobe to sleep on. He curls up every night after he has his half-and-half."

"Don't give him too much milk," ordered Christy. "Or cat treats. I don't want a fat and lazy cat when I get back."

"Too late, girlfriend. He's spoiled now. Gotta go. See ya." With that, the phone went dead leaving Christy cradling the receiver and feeling very much the outsider.

CHAPTER 16

By three o'clock, the death of Fremont Hobbs was officially confirmed as murder. It wasn't a difficult conclusion to come to: his head was bashed in repeatedly and, judging from the lack of defensive wounds, Fremont was either drunk or asleep at the time. Probably both.

The new investigation began at the only bar in the area, The Jerry-Rig. Fremont was a regular. Patrol deputies frequently encountered him stumbling along the side of the road, after a night of heavy boozing, and hauled him off to the Orange Cove jail for strong coffee and a chance to sleep it off.

Christy learned of Fremont's habits and habitat from the conversations of the deputies going on around her.

The man was apparently a fixture in the community, to be ridiculed and endured but accepted as part of the Burlap landscape. Not that he would be missed. Life would go on and sooner or later another of the Hobbs clan would come up the hill and claim rights to the homestead that wasn't in the family anymore.

Tapes flowed in from both homicides and landed on Christy's desk. Bit by bit, she was learning more about the town and its residents: their watering holes, lineage, addictions and failures. Life seemed to be intertwined among a handful of families, the original homesteaders in the area. The Jerry-'rig's owner Manny was related to Mona, the postmistress. School bus driver Emmy was married to Mona's son Jimmy. Hobbs Market was owned by Fremont's Aunt Sylvie. The geodesic house Christy had passed on the way up to Burlap was the creation of the Professor, a man ahead of his time in architecture and distribution of LSD. Folks talked freely in the interviews, willing to gossip about their neighbors. Several mentioned it was Fremont's partnership with the Professor in the late '60's was the reason he had a screw loose. It was the general opinion that, drugs, or no drugs, Fremont was always the diseased branch in the Hobbs family tree.

Burlap contained a more recent influx of residents, who the locals referred to as the flatlanders. These were outsiders who came to Burlap and built summer homes to escape the heat of the San Joaquin Valley floor. They were the butt of jokes by the Burlappers but tolerated because they brought money to the town. In the winter, their homes were fair game for the locals, requiring that the sheriff's department make good its motto: to protect and serve the absentee homeowners.

Also interviewed on the tapes were a handful of entrepreneurs. Sierra Real Estate had an A-frame sales office ready to sell property to more flatlanders. K. C. McGuire's Irish charm was evident on tape, sure to lure customers ready to get back to nature in modern homes. Cathy Fradenski operated a family health clinic. Trudy Meyers ran a bakery, and Potter's Wheel was the brainchild of Karyne Potter, who sold her overpriced creations to tourists.

All of the elementary school teachers carpooled from Orange Cove and seldom saw the parents of the children they taught. They had no idea who Fremont Hobbs or Lester Lehman were.

Strangest of all was Preacher, the fire-and-brimstone moral compass for the apathetic town. Pastor Kerman Adair used the detective's questions as an opportunity to rail against a town that was sure to go down like Sodom and Gonorrhea. Christy had to listen to the tape three times to clarify his phrasing. Yep, he was inadvertently referring to venereal disease, not the biblical city.

While the tapes were entertaining, detectives weren't any closer to solving the murders.

Which made Christy realize that she wasn't any closer to getting home.

ℰ∽ℰ∽

The cabin greeted her a bit more warmly when she when she was dropped off. The electricity was on and somebody had thought to bring an electric heater so she wouldn't burn the place down trying to light a fire. She tried the burners on the stove and flames appeared. There was a loaf of white bread on the counter with a jar of peanut butter, grape jelly, and Miracle Whip alongside. She found Campbell's soup in the cupboard: Alphabet Soup and Chicken with Stars. There were also cans of tuna, Beef-a-Roni and Spaghetti-O's, a box each of Co-Co Puffs and Lucky Charms. Apparently they'd sent a five-year-old to do the grocery shopping. Opening the refrigerator, she was pleased to discover bottled water, apples, a dozen eggs, milk, butter, and bologna.

Under the sink, she found a dented pot to warm the food and an iron skillet. Her eye caught sight of a bonus item: a tea kettle. Finally, civilization!

Christy went to her suitcase and brought out a plastic baggie containing several of her favorite teas. Irish Breakfast to wake up, jasmine to zen out, mint to get cozy, and chamomile to go to sleep. Never leave home without a stash of teabags was her motto. Chamomile was also good for headaches and Christy knew she was in store for a few if this job lasted much longer.

Dinner was scrambled eggs, two slices of buttered bread, washed down with milk. She would survive. Not in a healthy way, but she wouldn't starve, freeze, or be left in the dark.

With no TV and the limited number of paperbacks that she'd brought with her, Christy looked at the hours stretching ahead. What better way to figure out how this episode of her life would resolve itself but by casting her futurescope?

Christy kept copies of her own horoscope wheel pre-printed with the location of the planets when she was born. Having a prepped form ahead of time cut the process in half and stopped her from getting too lazy to glance into her own future from time to time. Now, she opened the ephemeris, a book containing rows of numbers based on NASA's computation of where the planets were each day.

She jotted down the ancient symbols for the planets and the signs along with the degrees where they were orbiting above.

Circles within circles, lines cutting through the wheel like wedges of a pizza—*jeez, a pepperoni pizza sounds good right now!*—the horoscope's familiarity had a calming effect on Christy. This was a piece of home. This was her personal universe. She felt herself getting centered, despite all the chaos of the last couple of days.

A recently acquired paperback, *Planets in Transit* by Robert Hand, was her latest find. It was a treasure tossed into the discard bin of the Central County Library. The copy she had, published over thirty-five years ago, was older than she was. When Christy freed the five-hundred-page book, still in good condition except for a curled corner and a bit of water damage, she knew the tome was going to answer many difficulties she had in grasping the elusive future.

She'd paid a dollar for the book. On Amazon, the hardbound version went for $117. Karma was looking after her and her wallet on that incredibly fruitful trip to the library. Gotta love Karma!

The first place Christy looked was obvious: the sixth house, employment. Yep, there was Neptune. *I should have known I'd find you here.* Flipping to the section on Neptune in the book, Christy scanned quickly. "Serious misunderstandings with employers, difficulty dealing with them." *Ya think?* It went on to mention involvement with work that was "subversive."

"I wouldn't call a murder investigation 'subversive,'" Christy muttered aloud. Maybe it was her attempt to get out of Burlap that was subversive. No, she'd made her intentions clearly known to anyone who would listen.

Saturn was acting pretty benign in the second house. No money flowing in, typical for a county employee. The book went on to explain that values were involved that went beyond money and material things, more in the area of psychological, spiritual, and moral values. "Learn what's really important," the description stressed.

Got it.

Pluto was too far ranging to worry about now. She

knew where she was in the planet's slow twenty year amble across her fourth house. Besides, who was taking Pluto seriously anymore since its demotion by astronomers?

On to Uranus. Christy didn't expect to find much since it was in the relationship house. Her growing romance with Rodrigo was solid. Sure, Uranus put tension between couples, but they'd never even had a spat yet. Hard to fight when he was off in some foreign country tracking down drug dealers—no time to argue when they had limited time together.

But the book indicated a possible relationship coming as a way to escape the daily routine. A wild, improbable and unstable love affair. Exciting stuff. *This sounds like Wolfe. Not gonna happen. Not even tempted.*

Mercury was also sitting in the seventh house. The planet usually moved at an uneven pace, streaking through the cosmos one minute, lingering the next. What caught her off guard was the admonishment to "clarify an issue with someone whom you are intimate." Was this talking about Lennie? The book also mentioned she would seek "intellectual stimulation and conversation, ranging from cheerful banter to spirited debate." Christy simply couldn't imagine any of the detectives would fulfill that prophecy.

The sun in the eighth house wasn't much help. The author talked about psychological health. Well, who could blame her if she went crazy stuck up here in the hills, dealing with ego-ridden detectives and dead bodies? Jupiter was right alongside the sun and not contributing much. Apparently, Christy was supposed to "pool her resources" with someone. Also "powerful and sweeping changes" were coming at her. *We'll see.*

She was already angry at Venus. Before the trip, Venus had assured her that it was a good time for a vacation. A trip "to a place you've never seen before" where she would "encounter something totally new." Once again, astrology was playing the old bait-and-switch. The planet also promised an attraction to someone "new, strange, and different." Christy wasn't looking for Prince Charming to come four-wheeling up the mountain anytime soon. And, if he did show up, she'd show him the door.

Finally, the wild card: Mars. Christy read with disdain that she should create a balance between her own self-interest and other people's interests. Not that she should subordinate herself—*you got that straight!*—but better to coordinate her needs with others. The problem, according to Mars, was finding a person she could work with. If she didn't find this person? The prediction was that she would be "more than usually resentful of group pressures."

Any planets in conflict? Oops, Saturn was in close contact with her natal Pluto. "You may have fewer resources available for doing what you want," read the book. "Focus available resources on more restricted and concentrated objectives."

"I have no idea what that means," Christy fumed. The "fewer resources" was probably her car. Her "concentrated objective" was to get the hell out of here.

The next line hit much too close to home: "Sometimes government or other officials will impose heavy burdens that greatly restrict your freedom of movement." Bingo!

Christy knew that if she'd looked more closely into her future prior to coming to Burlap, she might have had second thoughts on the whole trip. Now, it was too late to do much about it.

She noted that Uranus was perched directly opposite her natal Saturn. "Areas of your life that you think are reliable and dependable may cease to be, and you will be forced to make a lot of changes. It is likely you will feel a strong sense of uneasiness because you don't know quite what to expect next." Christy readily admitted she felt clueless in her work with homicide. "Uranus creates a sudden event that does not fit into the pattern of your life. This is happening now, largely through encounters with others or with enemies."

The homicide detectives are all my enemies right now.

It was excruciating to read line after line re-enforcing everything she was feeling about her situation. The horoscope seemed to be saying "Nah, nah, nah, look what you got yourself into."

The universe was taunting her.

Only one more planetary conflict, a biggie: Pluto squaring off with natal Saturn.

This can't be good, she thought, flipping to that section of the book.

As always, she was right. "During this transit you will have to withstand severe challenges to your way of life as it is set up now. You must adapt to the forces at work during this period for your own sake! You may feel like a victim of some massive external force beyond your control."

A victim. Yeah, that's exactly what she felt like. She read on. "During this transit some circumstance or situation will create forces that seem to push against you. You may feel very pressured to do something that you don't want to do at all, and you will probably put up tremendous resistance."

Did I try hard enough to get out of this? Christy now asked herself. It wasn't in her nature to buck the system. Well, not directly. Going around the rules was more her style.

The last part of the paragraph left her cold. "You may find that certain resources are no longer available and that you are forced more and more to fall back upon your own devices. This is part of the test of this transit."

I don't need any more damn tests, she wanted to scream at the universe. *Why are you picking on me?* Sometimes the horoscope felt like it was whacking her on the knuckles, instead of giving her any ways to fix the situation. Mentally and morally exhausted, Christy took a blissfully hot shower—they forgot to buy her soap, of course—brushed and flossed, and slipped under the quilt. The cabin was warm and reassuring after what she had just been through. If only that damn owl would go on day shift.

ℰↄℰↄ

The sound of the door rattling woke her. The first thought to flash in her mind was "bear." Then she jumped to "human," followed quickly by "killer." The lamp was too far to reach and would only let the threat know some-one was inside.

The full moon, shining through the window, helped her get her bearings. There was a solid piece of wood in the bin that she could use as a club, but getting to it would topple the rest of the woodpile and give away her presence. She looked over to the sink where the cast iron skillet was drying. Christy heard the door creak, then hit the logs used as a barrier and scrap them aside. She lunged out of bed and grabbed for the skillet. Before she could heft the heavy metal over her head, a voice called out "Don't move. I have a gun and I'll shoot."

CHAPTER 17

A flashlight blinded her. For a few seconds she felt like a burglar caught in the act. She tried to deflect the light by putting the skillet in front of her face. The weight of cast iron made her hand shake. That and fright.

"Who are you and what are you doing in my cabin?" The voice was calm, authoritative, and deep.

Christy peeked over the rim of the skillet. "Can you shine the light away from my face before you interrogate me?"

He obliged and snapped on the lamp. Christy laid the skillet on the counter and took a look at the man. He was tall, well-built, and had a mole on his lower left cheek that she found oddly sexy. Christy quickly surmised he was the forest ranger, back from fighting fires in Southern California.

"I thought you'd be gone longer," she said feebly.

"Are you a squatter? What happened to the lock I had on the door?"

"I work for the sheriff's department. They took the lock off your door and made me stay here." Christy paused then realized she had a question of her own. "Why don't you have an inside lock on your door?"

"Because I have a gun. People around here know better than to mess with me." As if to drive home his point, he put his gun on the counter. He looked at her suitcase with clothes spilling out. "Where's your car? I didn't see it parked outside or I would have had some idea you were in here."

Christy sat down on the bed and motioned for the ranger to take a seat in his home. "The lieutenant has it in impound so they can keep me prisoner up here. My name is Christy, by the way."

She stuck out her hand and he stood to shake it. "Brent Whatley. Are you a felon or something? Drunk driver?"

"No," Christy was appalled. Bad choice of words. "I'm a prisoner, figuratively speaking. There've been two murders and I happened to be the only office assistant up here visiting a friend. They won't let me go home until the murders are solved."

"So they decided to let you stay in my cabin." He ran

his fingers through his hair. "This is a problem."

Suddenly, Christy saw a glimmer of hope in the situation. "If you throw me out, maybe they'll let me go back to Coronita. I know they're too cheap to make me stay in the motel again."

"They let you sleep in that rat trap? Who did you piss off to get that kind of punishment?"

"I've been asking myself that question ever since I came up here."

He chuckled quietly. The sound reminded Christy of her father's reassuring laughter. She felt herself relaxing. The cabin became cozier with his presence.

"I've got my knapsack in my Jeep. Let me go get it and we'll talk about our situation." He got up.

"Do you drink tea?" Christy bounced up off the edge of the bed. "I can make us Irish Breakfast tea if you want."

He stopped and looked at her. "Is that regular tea, like Lipton's? I don't like green tea."

She smiled. "It's a black tea. You'll like it."

Before long, they were seated comfortably with hot mugs of tea warming their hands and conversation. Brent had never put milk in his tea before, a habit Christy had picked up from Grandma Good. Milk cut the tannin and left a creamy taste in the mouth. Grandma brought the tea habit with her as a war bride when she immigrated from England after the Great War.

Brent lifted his mug and saluted her. "You're a pretty

good hostess, seeing as how this was my place when I left."

"You're a good host to let me entertain you in your own home," Christy said, lifting her own mug in return.

They sipped, taking stock of each other. Christy explained about the murders and her temporary role. Brent nodded and looked concerned, enraged, and thoughtful at appropriate points in her narrative. For the first time since she'd arrived in Burlap, she felt like someone was actually listening to her. She wanted to talk all night.

A yawn on his part made her realize he was tired and ready to hit the sack. He seemed to realize he was winding down as well. Suddenly, the situation was awkward.

"How are we going to do this?" Brent asked, looking longingly at the single bed. He caught himself and stood up with a jolt. "I'll sleep in the Jeep."

"Oh, no, I can't kick you out of your own cabin. Besides, you'll get cold sleeping in the car." Christy meant what she said but hoped he wouldn't take her up on the offer. She had nowhere to go if he kicked her out.

He looked relieved. "I could get some blankets out of the car and make a pallet on the floor." He looked at her for permission.

"You can have the bed, I'll take the floor," she offered.

"What kind of a gentleman would I be if I let a lady sleep on the ground?" His eyes twinkled. He turned and went out to get the blankets.

Yes, he is a gentleman. Christy grabbed some cushions off the chair and laid them out across the room. She forfeited his feather pillow. When he returned, he looked with approval at the make-do bunk.

With few words, he stoked the fire in the potbelly stove to keep them warm through the night then took his shaving bag into the bathroom. Christy listened to him shower, brush his teeth, and gargle. *He's a hygienic gentleman. If he doesn't snore, he'll be the perfect roommate.*

"Goodnight, Christy," Brent said as he climbed under the blankets. "It's nice meeting you."

Christy felt warm, safe, and cared about. Her roommate didn't snore. Everything was going to be all right.

CHAPTER 18

Of course, Wolfe was the first to comment on her new and improved attitude.

They were riding to the substation. Thank goodness Brent slipped out of the cabin at dawn.

Once at the substation, Wolfe picked up paperwork and dropped off tapes, making sure she had plenty of work to keep her busy.

She gave him an amiable smile.

"Somebody got up on the right side of the bed this morning," he said, scrutinizing her. "I guess you've decided not to fight city hall."

"Things are just peachy keen," she replied. A grin played on her lips without prompting.

Wolfe cocked his head and continued to appraise. He

tried another jab. "Electricity and food sure improves your mood."

"Amazing what a few creature comforts can do for one's state of mind." Christy flipped her bangs away from her eyes, slipped a tape into the transcription machine, and adjusted the foot pedal. She positioned the ear buds into place.

Realizing he wasn't going to get a rise out of her, Wolfe shrugged and walked toward the door. He glanced back, giving her one more look, then shook his head in bafflement and left.

Christy took the plugs out of her ears and leaned back in the chair. She sat staring at the computer screen, savoring her thoughts about last night.

Now, having met Ranger Brent, the contents of the cabin fell into place. The quilt on the bed reflected his comforting presence. The books indicated intelligence, especially the volume of Henry David Thoreau. He seemed to pick up some of Thoreau's philosophy, as there were no extraneous objects in the cabin. Everything had a practical use and a precise placement. Very Walden Pondish.

On top of all that, he didn't snore. Christy realized she'd had the best sleep since arriving in Burlap.

Brent had snoozed on for a while as she showered and primped. Up to now, her lipstick stayed in her purse and she only wore tinted moisturizer for the SPF 30. Today she'd felt the necessity to brush a bit of blush on her cheeks and wear silver dangling earrings. Not for the homicide detectives—for herself.

I'm glowing.

The shrill ring of the telephone pulled her abruptly back to reality.

"Area 1 Substation. How can I help you?" she announced pleasantly.

"Did you find the tape?"

The mysterious female caller was checking in. Even though she was alone in the office, Christy lowered her voice.

"No. The evidence clerk said the answering machine was on the list but there was no tape inside."

"Didn't you think that was weird?" the woman gibed.

"Yeah, but I couldn't really push him. He's just the deputy who logs in evidence."

The woman let out an exasperated huff. "Don't you think it's a little stupid that the detectives didn't bother to follow up?"

Although Christy felt entitled to criticize the people she worked with, she was offended that an outsider took the same liberties. "Look, if you have a problem with the way the investigation is being conducted, why don't you give me your number, and I'll have one of the detectives talk to you. Better yet, contact Sheriff Nolan and lodge a complaint."

There was a long silence on the other end. "I can't

trust anyone in the sheriff's department." Her tone was suddenly humble and her voice shook.

Christy was caught off-guard. "Why are you saying that?"

"Because the deputy who worked with Lester had a reason to make that tape disappear."

Christy racked her brain to remember the name of the case agent. His was one of the early reports she'd transcribed. She could hear his voice in her head but the name eluded her.

The woman continued. "I heard what he said on the tape. He threatened to kill Lester."

"Please, this is not something I can deal with. You have to talk to somebody higher up," Christy begged.

A harsh laugh greeted her suggestion. "I know how law enforcement works. This is a cover-up. They protect their own."

"Oh, come on. Don't go telling me there's some conspiracy going on." Christy quickly wrote the woman off as a 5150, a nutcase, certifiable.

"You don't believe me?"

Christy exploded. "If you're so paranoid, why do you keep calling me?"

"You're the only one I can trust."

The women shared a long silence.

"You have to ask Lester's handler why he took the tape. I think the killer is right under everybody's nose."

Click.

CHAPTER 19

Christy hated the woman. Her paranoid theories, her ridicule of the men Christy worked for, her accusations. Christy hated her because Ms. Anonymous planted doubts in her mind. Christy couldn't stop hearing the words. They couldn't be erased like a transcription tape. Or an answering machine cassette.

Christy opened up the investigation files in the computer and scrolled through the earliest interviews. The case agent was Narcotics Detective B. Razulo.

There wasn't much in the report. Razulo had busted Lester Lehman six months before on charges of dealing cocaine and offered him a choice: go to trial and spend time in jail or switch sides and become a confidential informant, or CI.

Lehman was a small-time street dealer of no importance or real threat. This was his first arrest. He was stupid enough to sell to Razulo, a random act of commerce that backfired.

Razulo recruited him in hopes that Lehman would lead him to a supplier. The CI contract was standard: X amount of monitored drug buys, agree to wear a wire, check in daily, be available for undercover operations 24/7, no funny stuff or it was Go To Jail, Do Not Pass Go, Do Not Collect A Clean Record.

Lehman, according to Razulo, turned out to be an excellent snitch. He introduced the undercover detective to his connections, resulting in several arrests. As with many informants, Lehman became so enamored with his new role that he began to believe he was a deputy of sorts, working for the sheriff. His misguided enthusiasm, Razulo indicated in his report, made Lehman more of a risk than a reliable player in the high-stakes game of drug dealing.

When Lehman failed to return Razulo's calls, the case agent was concerned. Razulo was responsible for his snitch and ultimately had to answer to the sergeant and lieutenant for Lehman's behavior. Razulo paid a visit to check on Lehman at the trailer the narc team acquired for the duration of the contract, courtesy of Central County. Tax dollars at work. Homicide detectives were at the scene upon Razulo's arrival.

End of report.

No mention of a tape.

Christy faced a conundrum. She wasn't sure she was in a position to annoy the investigators with accusatory questions. Her job was to stay out of the way and just do the scut work as she was told. The detectives made the point very clear that she was just a body with office skills available to do their bidding.

On the other hand…

On the other hand, her involvement in earlier cases resulted in solving crimes of kidnapping, killings, and conspiracies. Not that Christy ever received any credit. She could have been fired for her actions. Not that she ever intended to get sucked any closer to law enforcement than typing reports and fielding phone calls. Let others get their thrills carrying a gun and kicking in doors. All Christy wanted was a 9-to-5 job, an adequate paycheck, and health benefits.

Yet, once again, Karma saw fit to throw a curve ball her way in the form of an anonymous phone call.

What she should do was pretend the call never happened. What she wanted to do was talk the situation over with Lennie. Lennie had been her wingman in the past, getting them both in trouble and still finding ways to escape intact. Lennie was the brains in their crazy schemes as well as the brawn. Somehow, Christy was always the lackey. These were the roles they seemed destined to repeat time and again.

'*You need to pursue the lead.*'

The voice intruded her thoughts. Ah, Celeste was psychically dialing in with her opinion of the situation.

Christy's older sister was born with a high degree of what was termed "The Family Gift." She could read thoughts even from a distance. The sisters had communicated this way all their lives, a game they played without realizing there was anything special going on. Grandma Good was the one who figured it out—after all, she was a highly honed player in mind reading. As was her Irish grandmother before her. The Gift was handed down through female genes, regularly skipping a generation. Christy's mother was clueless, too self-absorbed to pay much attention.

Celeste channeled her gift as a Dominican nun in the belief that God was working through her. Grandma Good used her powers to increase her odds when gambling. Christy found her own psychic ability was strongest when she cast horoscopes.

While Celeste nominated herself as Christy's conscience, a sort of Jiminy Cricket in a black and white habit, Grandma Good was more interested in Christy's sex life. A little too interested, as far as Christy was concerned. Dolly Good had the habit of taking vicarious pleasure in Christy's relationship with Rodrigo Murietta. Their intrusion inhibited Christy up to a point, but she was learning to block their ESP intervention.

Instead of acknowledging this unwanted "gift," Christy kept it under wraps. People she worked with thought she was strange enough with the astrology side-line. She didn't need them questioning her sanity as well.

But ESP was useful as a communication tool, apparently more reliable than cell phones in her current situation. '*Nice of you to weigh in,*' Christy telegraphed back to her sister.

'*I sensed your conflict,*' Celeste replied from the convent in Springfield, Illinois.

'*I can't get cell phone reception, but you're coming through loud and clear.*'

'*God works in mysterious ways. Like a satellite dish.*'

'*Who said nuns don't have a sense of humor?*'

If Celeste was monitoring her thoughts, was Grandma Good also on the party line?

'*No,*' replied Celeste. '*She's in Vegas, gambling. Too many distractions. She's winning on the slot machines. I think she's cheating by using ESP to locate the ones ready to hit.*'

'*Good to know.*'

'*Back to your situation. Perhaps you were sent to the mountains to be a bridge between the woman and the detectives,*' Celeste suggested.

'*Do you believe her story?*'

'*I sense that she's being truthful. The rest is your area of expertise.*'

'*You're reading my thoughts so you know where I'm going with this, right?*'

'To the source, I hope. It's the honest thing to do. Oh, and make up with Lennie. She's important in your life. As for this new man—'

Christy quickly cut her off. *'Thanks for checking in, Celeste. Gotta run.'*

'I'll pray for you.'

'You do that.'

Christy reached for the sheriff's department directory and looked up the number for the narc unit. With the blessing of her sister, she punched in the number.

"SID," came a crisp, no-nonsense greeting.

Christy recognized it as shorthand for Special Investigation Division. "I'd like to speak to Detective Razulo, please," she requested.

"Who's calling?" The secretary sounded suspicious, like a pit bull guarding her domain. Maybe the attitude came with the job.

"Christy Bristol. I'm working on the homicide case in Burlap."

"Oh. Yeah." The voice hinted she'd been briefed. In fact, Christy got the impression the narc secretary knew more about the case than she did. The woman sounded seasoned. "How's it going up in the foothills? I heard they picked you up on the fly. You work out at the Area 3 Substation, right?"

Smug.

"Is Detective Razulo in? Or, should I leave a message on his voice mail?" Two could play this game.

The woman seemed to feel it was her prerogative to be a barrier between callers and the detectives. Christy knew secretaries did power plays with what little authority they had in their jobs.

Without warning, Christy found herself on hold.

At least, she hoped she was on hold and not disconnected.

Finally, an impatient voice said, "Razulo."

"Detective Razulo, this is Christy Bristol."

"Yeah?" Obviously, her name didn't ring any bells.

"I'm the one typing reports for Homicide up in Burlap," Christy persisted.

"Oh. Yeah." Recognition.

Christy began to doubt her decision to confront the detective.

"I was wondering—" She hesitated, trying to find a diplomatic way to ask. "Did you forget to list the answering machine tape on the evidence sheet?"

Christy braced for a barrage of insults for questioning the detective's professionalism. Instead, Razulo lowered his voice to a whisper. "Why?"

"I was afraid I'd forgotten to type it in the report. I wanted to correct the error."

She waited while Razulo digested this information. Would he confirm the anonymous accuser's suspicions?

What seemed like a stand-off ended with Razulo asking, "Have you gone to anyone else about this? The captain or a homicide detective?"

Christy's pulse raced. "No, I wanted to first confirm with you that the tape was misplaced."

"If I come up there, will you be alone in the office?"

Christy was caught off-guard. "I don't know. Detectives come and go all day long."

"No, all the brass are going to be at headquarters all afternoon briefing the sheriff about the case. The detectives are going to take advantage and be doing long lunches or catching up on other stuff in their offices. Doesn't anybody tell you what's going on?" he asked.

"Not really," Christy admitted.

Razulo came up with a plan. "Can you meet me somewhere for lunch?"

"The detectives took my car," Christy replied. "I can't go anywhere and, anyway, they don't let me take off for lunch. I have to stay in the office and watch the phones."

"What are you—a hostage?"

"Something like that."

Razulo let loose with a few choice expletives, describing the homicide team. He calmed and said, "I'm taking you to lunch. Have dispatch notify your immediate boss that you are taking a lunch break. By the time she gives him the message, you'll already be back. I'll see you in thirty."

Christy sank back in her chair and grinned. So, that's the way the game was played. If anybody wanted to complain, she could just say Detective Razulo requested time to discuss the case with her and insisted they meet away from the office. Let him explain his instructions. She was just doing what she was told by someone with more seniority and authority. Just doing her job.

Razulo pulled up in a green mini-cab pickup truck. The undercover vehicle was dusty and dented and had obviously been on a few drug busts in its time. Christy left the office and locked the door behind her. Razulo leaned across the passenger seat and opened the door. With an awkward step on the door frame, Christy took a seat in the truck.

Razulo was slightly built with light brown wiry hair. The only clue to his heritage was a Roman nose that took up a good portion of his face. As a physical feature, it was a nose to remember. The rest of his face accommodated the appendage with small eyes, high forehead, and tawny facial hair.

In the car were two bags of treats from Rocko's Tacos and colas. This was his idea of "going out to lunch"? Not that she expected a four-star restaurant or even a splurge at Ronnie's Roadhouse for chicken fried steak, but this? Razulo hadn't bothered to ask if she liked faux Mexican food or her drink preference.

They took off in a cloud of dust, the detective sparing no time for pleasantries. When he decided they were far enough from civilization, he pulled the truck onto a dirt road and stopped under the deep shade of an oak.

He shoved one of the bags into her hands and pulled

out an over-sized burrito from his bag. "Who told you about the tape?" he asked while simultaneously chewing.

Christy, not wanting to give up her source so early in the game, said, "I knew the old answering machines used cassettes. My parents had one like that years ago. But when I transcribed evidence listed in the report, I didn't see the cassette mentioned."

"If you thought there was a problem, why didn't you ask the homicide detectives?" Razulo honed in on her, his eyes narrowed like a wary rat. "Why did you call me?"

Christy put bits of fallen lettuce back into her taco. "I'm just covering all the bases," she said, on the defensive.

"You mean covering your ass," he shot back.

"Yeah? What are you covering up?" Now her temper blazed. "All those calls to your informant and suddenly there's no trace of any of your messages. I think investigators might wonder if you said something incriminating on the machine." She threw the greasy taco back in the bag and turned away to look out the window and gain her composure.

She heard a long gurgle as Razulo washed the mouthful of tortilla and beans down with his soda.

When his throat was clear, he asked, "Are you accusing me of stealing the tape?"

Literally backed into the corner of the front seat, Christy decided to go on the offensive. She turned to face the narc. "Did you?"

Razulo's Italian temper erupted like Mt. Vesuvius. He let loose with a string of profanities. The detective repeatedly slammed his fist on the dashboard. Christy realized the cussing wasn't directed at her but at his own demons.

"I knew this shit would come back on me. Stupid, stupid, stupid," he railed.

His outburst was followed by deadly silence.

Finally, Christy ventured to ask, "What was on the tape?"

"Nothing." Razulo looked at her, pleading for her to believe him. "I left a stupid message. He wasn't answering any of my calls so I said I was going to kill him."

Startled, Christy said, "That could be misinterpreted, don't you think?"

Razulo wearily shook his head. "I just said it to make a point. I wouldn't have really killed him. Although there were times when I wanted to kick his lazy ass."

Tough love? Is that how a case officer operates?

"I didn't steal the tape," Razulo finally confessed. "I wanted to. Just after I made the threat, some woman picked up the phone and told me I was too late, Lester was already dead. I knew that if my sergeant found out what I'd said, he'd kick me out of the unit."

"What did you do?"

"I tried to get to Lester's place first so I could erase my last message. By the time I got there, deputies were swarming the crime scene."

Unethical but understandable. Christy knew that, in law enforcement, saving one's butt came first. Consequences could be dealt with later.

"The woman must have been Lester's lay. Hell, she probably killed him. I have to find out who she is and pull her in for questioning." Having convinced himself he was off the hook, Razulo reached for the ignition.

Christy covered his hand with her own to stop him from turning the key. "She didn't kill him."

Razulo pulled his hand away, leaned back in the seat, and studied Christy. "You know something?"

She couldn't look him in the eye, so she stared down at her hands. There was hot sauce on her fingers. "She called the office," Christy began. "She told me there was a cover-up. Basically, she pointed the finger at you. I didn't believe her," she hastily added, "but when I couldn't locate the tape, I felt I had to check out her accusations."

"She took the tape," Razulo confidently stated. "She's just trying to throw us off track. You have to tell me who she is and how to find her."

"I can't." Christy found a napkin and distractedly cleaned off her fingers. "She's called twice but doesn't give any info, just harps at me to investigate. I don't want to be in this position."

"Right, right. Not your problem." Razulo chewed the fringe of his mustache while he searched for a solution.

"Next time she calls, route the call to me. Better yet, let me give you my cell number."

"You're the last person she'll talk to," Christy pointed out. "Remember, she thinks you're the one who killed her boyfriend."

"Try anyway," Razulo insisted. "Tell her I'm in her corner. I wouldn't have hurt Lester. I mean, he was a royal pain and not too bright, but a really good guy—for a drug dealer."

Christy nodded her assent but she was pretty sure what the caller's reaction would be.

When Razulo dropped her back at the substation, she forgot to thank him for the meal. Not a big deal—all in all, it was a pretty crappy lunch.

CHAPTER 20

Christy got back to the cabin early, after one of the deputies showed up to take her home. Ranger Brent wasn't around but signs of his presence were evident. His razor was lined up with hers on the sink. He preferred bar soap to her vanilla scented shower gel. Shined boots were lined up by the potbelly stove. The cabin smelled fresh, aired out. Cobwebs were gone from the wood beams and what few surfaces needed dusting were debris free.

Ranger Brent was all spit and polish. Now, if he could only cook…

The door opened and Brent came in, carrying an ice chest and a grocery bag. He was dressed in a faded orange T-shirt that showed off his broad chest and muscular arms to advantage. The logo "Tomkats Grille, Old Koloa Town, Kaua'i" was emblazoned on the front and silhouettes of three cats on a fence with a yellow moon in the background decorated the back.

"I like the T-shirt," Christy commented. "You've been to Kaua'i?"

"A couple of times." The ranger shrugged. "My folks have a time share. The island isn't as crowded or commercial as Oahu. Lots of great snorkeling and fishing. Speaking of which—" He opened the ice chest, pulled out a freshly caught fish, and held it up by the tail. "I brought dinner."

Christy didn't exactly know fish varieties and the only fish she could cook were fish sticks. "Do I have to clean it or anything?" she asked tentatively.

"Nope. I'll scale it, gut it, and barbecue it. All you have to do is make a salad." He pointed to the brown grocery sack.

As Brent went outside to fire up a small hibachi, Christy unloaded the groceries: two kinds of lettuce, butter, and bib, radishes, mushrooms, cucumbers, tomatoes, garlic croutons, and red-wine-vinegar dressing. Nice.

Of course, he would eat healthy, she thought as she washed and separated the lettuce leaves. She also noticed he didn't smoke and there wasn't beer in the cooler. This was a man who respected his body and knew to keep it well-tuned for the tough job of fighting fires and hiking through the national forest. Brent was a throw-back to the mountain men who lived with nature, understood the wilderness, and respected its moods.

The table—large enough for one, a tight fit for two—was set with the few pieces of cutlery and the only two plates in the cabin. If she'd known they were going to do the fine-dining thing, she would have picked some wildflowers—not that there was a vase around or any place on the tiny table to put them. There were, surprisingly enough, cloth napkins neatly tucked in with the dish towels. Plain white but obviously ironed, and totally unexpected.

"Nice." Brent came in, bearing two pieces of grilled fish on a piece of metal that looked somewhat like a cookie sheet. He carefully lifted the fish with a spatula and set it on her plate.

"There's no room for that salad bowl," Christy said.

Brent pulled a chair out and waited for her to sit down. He then picked up both plates and forks, walked over to the counter, and proceeded to dole out large portions on each plate. "You make a great salad," he commented with a wink.

Christy felt her face redden. Blushing? She was blushing? Suddenly she realized that she was feeling just a tiny bit shy with the whole situation.

Brent dug into the food with enthusiasm. Christy carefully examined the fish.

"You don't like fish?" he asked.

"I'm just leery about bones," she answered.

"I de-boned it." He smiled. "You don't eat much fish, do you?"

Busted. "I try," Christy said. "I know it's healthy and all, but honestly, it stinks up the house something awful."

"You'll like this," Brent said. "Nothing like fresh-caught trout cooked within an hour of leaving the stream." He waited for her to take a bite.

Christy put a small piece on her fork and into her mouth. The fish was heavenly. Flaky, no pungent smell of fish that she expected. Maybe all she'd eaten before was salt-water fish. Bones forgotten, she cut a larger chunk.

Brent grinned, pleased with his conquest. "What did I tell you?"

As he continued eating, Christy was acutely aware that under the table their knees were touching. Not in a flirty way, just forced together by the small space. The sensation wasn't unpleasant, which didn't surprise Christy, but felt very intimate.

In fact, the entire scene was romantic: dinner in an isolated cabin tucked away in the forest with a great look-ing guy who not only caught the food but cooked and served it.

Yes, something right out of a Harlequin novel or chick flick.

"Penny for your thoughts."

Christy abruptly pulled out of dream state. "What?"

"You had this very contented look on your face. I

know the fish is good, but I seemed to lose you for a moment."

Christy laughed to stall. "I guess I was just thinking that this was the first good experience I've had since I drove up here."

"Why? What's been going on? Besides the murders, I mean."

Christy raised an eyebrow. "Okay, let's start with that. I shouldn't even be up here. I'm not part of the homicide team. I came up to visit a friend and the detectives sort of kidnapped me."

"Can they do that?"

"Oh, the sheriff can do anything he wants. I was convenient, a pawn that can type and has to take orders. I wasn't given a choice." She could feel anger rising up. "On top of that, my friend and I had a major blow-out over her jerk of a boyfriend. To get back at me she stole all the Dr Pepper in a 50-mile radius."

Brent choked on a crouton. Christy was offended that he was laughing at her, but then she realized how ridiculous the situation must sound to him. She started laughing, too.

Brent took a swig of water to clear his throat. "You have suffered," he agreed.

"More than you know. I miss my cat. I miss my apartment. The woman I was training at the substation is so good, everyone's forgotten about me. I want my life back."

Brent put his hand over hers. "It must be hard. But can't you enjoy yourself while you're stuck here? People travel all over the world to come see the Sierra Nevadas, the giant Sequoias, Yosemite. There are worse places to be stranded."

Christy only half heard his plea. She was fighting the strange reaction of his hand covering hers.

"I know this isn't a vacation for you," he continued. He crooked his neck to try to catch her down-turned eyes. "And this isn't a resort. Burlap is just a nothing town tucked away and forgotten in the foothills."

Christy felt his fingers go under her chin and lift her face. He leaned forward to look into her eyes.

"Consider what you've got here. Clean air, the smell of pine, solitude. You can commune with the land, wake up with the sun and the sound of the birds, go to sleep without a TV or an alarm clock. Can't you appreciate all that surrounds you?"

Words. That's all Christy heard. She was mesmerized by his gentle, brown, knowing eyes.

"Besides—" He laughed, pulling away and going back to his salad. "—you sure add something special to this rustic old cabin."

❧❧❧

Not until after the dishes were washed and put away did Christy realize that there was a problem. Brent had gone out to get more firewood to take the chill off the night. When he came back in with an armful of wood, she waited until he set it down and began positioning logs and twigs inside the pot belly stove. Soon he had a blaze going. Leave it to a firefighter to know how to light a good fire.

"I've taken your home away from you," she hesitantly began. "I need to find another place to stay. Or rather, the sheriff needs to find me decent accommodations. I can't keep imposing. You've been very understanding and all, but hospitality only goes so far."

"You're going to have a tough time finding anyplace else to stay." He got up from the fireplace and sat down next to her on the bed. "I can't recommend the only hotel in town."

"The Franklin Inn. Yes, I've been there and you're right, I would never recommend it to my worst enemy."

"They should have a sign: 'Ben Franklin slept here. We haven't changed the sheets since.'"

They both laughed. When the moment passed, a somber mood replaced it.

"I don't really mind you staying here," Brent said quietly.

"You have a great place. It reflects who you are."

"And who am I, Christy?"

Okay, awkward. She jumped up and went to the bookshelf. "You're a guy who reads Thoreau in the forest."

She pulled the book down from the shelf and handed it to him.

"Have you read Henry David?" he asked, taking the book from her.

"Oh, so you're on a first-name basis?"

He laughed as he turned pages. "Yeah, H.D. and I hang out together. We have lots of time together on cold winter nights."

"I read his book 'Walden' in school. Well, sort of. Parts. The good parts, I hope."

"They're all good." Brent stroked the book as if greeting an old friend. "'Nature will bear the closest inspection. She invites us to lay our eyes level with her smallest leaf and take an insect's view of the world.'"

"That's beautiful."

"His words go so much deeper than what's written on the page."

"You sound like the book is your bible."

"Yeah, I guess I think of his work as a text for living. He was a man with a grasp on what's important in the world and in a man's soul. In fact, he said it best: 'A truly good book teaches me better than to read it. I must soon lay it down and commence living on its hint. What I began by reading, I must finish by acting.'"

"Very zen," Christy commented.

Brent laughed. "He was the first hippie. And an environmentalist. He should have lived in the 1960s or '70s."

"No, people would just say he was on LSD."

The diversion had worked, but the question was still in the room.

"What do you think we ought to do with my living arrangements?" Christy asked.

A slight grin etched Brent's face. "Nothing for tonight. I think it's too dark for me to pitch a tent for you in the woods. Plus, I'm not sure how you'd handle owls for company. They can be a hoot."

"Ouch. That pun hurt."

Brent got up and pulled the blanket from the bed. He proceeded to make a pallet on the floor just as he had the night before.

"Look, I'll take the floor tonight. You need to sleep in your own bed."

"Are you kidding? What kind of host would I be letting a lady sleep on the floor like a dog? Besides," he said, tossing down his jacket for a pillow, "I've slept on worse fighting fires. Nothing puts you to sleep faster than a hard day, smoke in your eyes, and a bed of pine needles."

Sometime in the night, Christy heard Brent get up and leave the cabin. She heard his Jeep rev up and the crunch of gravel. Puzzled, Christy hazily wondered if he was making some sort of rounds to check for fires. Or, maybe there was a woman in town waiting for a booty call.

She turned over and went back to sleep. Whatever the reason, it was his business and not hers to pry.

CHAPTER 21

Brent gave her a ride to work the next morning. Christy had nearly forgotten about the vanishing act in the middle of the night. She decided that if he wanted to tell her, he would.

As they pulled up to the station, a few vehicles were already parked in the gravel lot.

"Are you late?" Brent glanced at his watch. Seven forty-five. "I thought you opened up for business at eight."

Christy noted two patrol cars and Razulo's truck. "Something must be going on," she said.

"I can pick you up later."

She nodded and hurried inside.

Wolfe and Razulo were kicking back in office chairs,

one of them being hers. Deputy Espinoza was leaning over the counter, jingling a set of keys. He straightened up when Christy walked in.

"Up," she commanded Wolfe.

"Before you get comfortable, how 'bout making coffee? We got you a machine," he said.

"How about learning to make it yourself," she snapped.

"Ew, somebody got up off the wrong side of the bed this morning," Wolfe teased. "Did the ranger take the covers? Did he hog the pillow?"

How could news travel that fast? Christy set her purse down on the desk and stood, hand on hip, waiting for Wolfe to vacate the seat.

"I guess the job got just a little more interesting for you, huh?" he continued to needle. "No complaints about being stuck up here now? No whining to go home?"

"Come on, Wolfe. Give it a break," Razulo said as he jerked his buddy out of the chair. "Let her get back to work." He looked shyly at Christy. "I'll get a pot of coffee going," he said and disappeared to the back room.

"Thanks," Christy called out to him. She sat down at the chair, irritated that the seat was still warm. Leave it to Wolfe to destroy a perfectly good morning.

Wolfe pointed to paperwork on the desk. "Hit and run. Occurred last night at approximately 0200 hours. They're going to need the report at Headquarters ASAP."

Christy fingered the notes. "I thought I was here to

work with homicide. Aren't there office assistants in records who can handle this?"

Shrugging, Wolfe said, "Sure. But you're here and you're convenient. Besides, there's nothing new going on with the murder investigations right now."

Razulo appeared with a mug of hot coffee. He carried a packet of powdered creamer and three packets of sugar and set it on the desk.

"Thanks." She reached for the brew and inhaled deeply. Mt. Rainer, Lennie's coffee. Brewed a little too strong. She proceeded to doctor it up with the creamer and two sugars. She didn't want to insult Razulo by using the sweetener she kept in her purse.

"What's with all this waiting on her hand and foot?" Wolfe demanded. "Aren't you going to serve the rest of us?"

"Get your own coffee, Wolfe," Razulo snapped.

"I'll get us some." Espinoza eagerly ducked out to avoid the pissing contest going on between the two men.

"Black," Wolfe called out to Espinoza's retreating back.

"My handwriting is a little hard to make out," Razulo apologized. "I didn't have time to put the report on tape. Sorry."

He was right; his penmanship looked like the Rosetta stone of report writing. She was going to spend half a day trying to decipher the hieroglyphics.

Espinoza returned with two Styrofoam cups of coffee. He handed one cup to Wolfe and shifted impatiently, eager to leave.

"You're the one who found the victim?" Christy asked, looking from the report to Razulo.

"Yeah. He was laid out in the middle of Road 18, near Welfare Flats. Mangled pretty bad."

"Bro, what were you doing out so late?" Wolfe asked.

Apparently, the question had occurred to him at the same time as Christy.

"Someone dropped a dime with info on Lester's case. Wanted to meet me up in the hills."

"Pretty dangerous going up there in the middle of the night without backup," Wolfe pointed out.

"Naw, I found the body at 0500 hours. The coroner put the time of death at 0200," Razulo explained. "What, you think I don't know how to handle myself in the field?"

"Shouldn't you have relayed the call to homicide? They're handling the Lehman case." Wolfe wasn't going to let it slide.

"Sure, wake up Captain Hillard and Lieutenant Brandt at home before they're out of bed? I'd lose rank for that. Besides, Lester was my snitch. I'm invested in this case."

He glanced over at Christy. She caught his meaning right away.

"Whatever, dude." Wolfe turned away from Razulo.

"So, tell us, Christy, how's Mr. DEA going to feel about you shacking up with Mr. Forest Ranger?"

Christy whirled around in the swivel chair. "I don't know, Wolfe. He'll probably wonder why the county is too cheap to find a better place for me to stay."

"Yeah, well, you take what you can get. Right?" He snickered, adding intended insult to the words.

"Let's get out of here and let her work," Razulo said.

He brushed past Wolfe, making sure to add an aggressive bump between shoulders on the way to the door. The aggressive move wasn't ignored as Wolfe chased after him. Espinoza hurried to catch up.

Christy could hear the men exchanging angry words in the parking lot. She was *so* over the posturing of deputies, like roosters in a cockfight. The rivalry in law enforcement between departments, between agencies, between ranks seemed a tedious waste of time and energy. While the men aggressively one-upped each other, office assistants like herself kept the system running.

Being the center of the tug-of-war between Homicide and Narcotics might seem flattering to some office assistants, but Christy was tired of her role as a pawn in the department warfare.

She wished Sergeant Traynor had tried a little harder to insist on his rights as her boss to keep her at her assigned position.

Perhaps, with just a little resistance and more of a fight on his part, the homicide brass would have decided the battle wasn't worth the energy and gotten one of their own office workers up here.

Everyone seemed satisfied with the status quo except herself. Being displaced was bad enough; being heckled for the "sinful" arrangement of sharing the cabin with its owner was uncalled for. Oh, like she had a choice!

Or, she mused, maybe Wolfe was pissed that his scheme had taken a turn in her favor.

Christy played with the possibility that Wolfe's reaction might be based less on spite than jealousy. As she sipped the cooled coffee, she thought about their "blissful" days as a couple when he was a patrol deputy at the Coronita Substation.

They'd known each other for two years, saw each other at work nearly every day. She'd been twenty-six, already working at the sheriff's department since high school graduation. Staying under the radar of the testosterone-driven deputies wasn't hard. With her conservative clothes, thick glasses, mousy-brown hair, and lack of skills with make-up, Christy knew she hadn't exactly been a male-magnet.

Wolfe slowly lured her out of her shyness, plying her with 32 ounce Dr Peppers from the nearby "stop-and-rob." The extra attention started out as a harmless flirtation, but she was an easy target. After six months of dating—and some pretty incredible sex—Wolfe suggested he move into her second-floor apartment in the Victorian house on Muscat Road.

His argument was sound: the apartment was close to the substation, he wouldn't have to make the twenty-mile trek to his place in Kearny, plus he could help with the rent. The fact that her apartment cost considerably less than what he paid for a studio pad in the city was certainly part of the attraction in their relationship.

For Christy, the decision carried much more impact. First, there were her parents. While not the morality police, her father was from the South and the idea of his daughter living in sin went against his idea of the behavior of a gentleman with good intentions. Christy decided the best thing was not to tell him. He never visited her in Coronita, so discovery wasn't a concern.

Her mother figured out the change in living arrangements right away. At first, Christy simply mentioned she had a new roommate without being gender-specific. A surprise visit from Mom removed all doubts. Regina Bristol spotted a man's razor as well as Christy's birth control pills when she covertly inspected the medicine cabinet. Instead of being appalled, she sighed with relief that her daughter finally had a beau. Yes, that was the word she used—beau. Not lover, not "significant other," but a prequel to "husband." Plus, Regina loved a good secret.

There was no hiding from Celeste or Grandma Good, yet another instance when the psychic connection complicated Christy's life. As expected, Celeste objected on religious grounds, and no argument Christy brain-waved back could change her Sister sister's mind. Christy finally cut the nun off by promising to sew a red "A" on her sweater. Celeste stayed incommunicado for three months.

Grandma Good was a much larger interference. Dolly Good was quite frisky in her heyday, blaming it on World War II and the influx of American soldiers in England. Even without a major war, Christy felt her grandmother would have found some outlet for her escapades, short of working in a brothel. Grandma Good, foiled by Regina's honorable intent of marriage and Celeste's religious calling, pinned all her hopes on Christy. For Dolly Good, having a man move in with her granddaughter topped the fall of the Berlin Wall.

There was also the problem of the landlady and the other renter at the Muscat house. Mrs. Alcorn wasn't the prying type, but even a near-sighted, partially deaf senior could detect the added bedroom activity going on overhead. Mr. Macial, in the attic apartment, approved of her roommate—perhaps a little too much.

And then, out of nowhere, Wolfe dumped her. On her thirtieth birthday. Timing was never his strong point.

The blast of the telephone pulled her out of reflections better forgotten.

"Area One Substation," Christy announced.

"Did you find the tape?"

Caught off-guard, Christy snapped, "No."

"Told you. That scumbag narc took off with it to protect his ass."

"Listen," Christy shot back. "I talked to the detective and he's as worried as you are. He didn't kill Lester. At one point, he pointed the finger at you. He thinks you were the one who picked up the telephone. Maybe you took off with the tape."

"Bullshit."

There was a long silence on both ends.

"I'm going to hang up now," Christy said.

"No, wait." The woman suddenly sounded vulnerable, dropping the tough act. "I just want your guys to find out who killed Lester. And Hobbs. These were my friends and somebody is knocking them off for no reason."

"Then you have to talk to Detective Razulo," Christy insisted.

"How can I trust him? How can I trust anybody? Maybe they want me to shut up or they'll find a way to shut me up." She sounded desperate.

"Razulo says he's in your corner."

"Yeah, right."

Frustrated with trying to get through to this woman, Christy erupted. "No matter what you think, there's a bond between detectives and the informants they work with. They both put their lives on the line, trying to keep the rest of us safe. Razulo and Lester were a team. He's as upset as you are. You've got to believe that." Christy paused, hoping she'd made her case. "You have to talk to Razulo. I can transfer you to him right now."

"No." The woman was adamant. "I will only talk to you. If he has something to say to me, let him tell you."

"That's not how the system works," Christy explained. "There's a chain of command and I'm at the bottom. Do you get what I'm saying? I'm not supposed to investigate. I'm expected to type reports, keep my opinions to myself, and be invisible. If I start passing messages, the brass will come after me. Big time."

"You're the only one I trust."

Caught in the quandary of being flattered by a woman clearly using her, Christy caved. "I'm not included in your conspiracy theory—lucky me. But I can't play this role you want to put me in." She couldn't keep the exasperation out of her voice.

"I'll call you when I feel it's safe."

Click.

CHAPTER 22

Christy left a message on Razulo's voice mail to let him know there'd been another phone call. She kept the words cryptic in case anyone monitored his messages. *Now who's being paranoid,* she thought.

She'd barely had time to look at the hit-and-run report when detectives rushed into the substation. Captain Hillard and Lieutenant Brandt led the pack. As the tornado swirled around her, Christy hunkered down and waited for someone to fill her in.

The captain snatched the paperwork off her desk and read through the report, passing each handwritten page off to his lieutenant as he finished reading.

"This isn't a typical hit-and-run," Hillard announced.

"Not unless the driver backed up to admire his hand-iwork," Brandt jeered.

The detectives laughed appreciatively.

"Do you think this is funny?" Hillard asked, address-ing the group. The snickering stopped.

"You have to admit, it's kinda funny," Brandt smirked.

"Shut up," Hillard ordered. "Somebody make a pot of coffee."

"That's what we've got a secretary for," a detective pointed out.

Hillard shot the detective an irritated look. "She's got actual work to do. You just volunteered."

All eyes were suddenly focused on Christy. She shifted uneasily in the chair.

"Have you started typing the report yet?" Hillard asked.

"No sir. I just received it from Detective Razulo."

"Razulo again." He sighed. "There's going to be an addendum to the report. I've got one of my people writ-ing it up right now. This new info states that the felony manslaughter is upgraded to PC 187."

"Somebody backed over ol' Slepski and took another run at him," Brandt chortled.

Hillard turned on the lieutenant. "Are you going to take this seriously? There's a man dead out there."

"Come on, Captain. It's Slepski. He's been nearly run over every time he leaves the bar. Hell, I've found him sleeping on the side of the road after a bender and nearly hit him myself."

A murmur of agreement spread among the men.

"Stop being a jerk. Under the circumstances, we have to consider that this might be in conjunction with the other murders we're investigating," Hillard said.

Conviction was absent from his words.

"The theory's a stretch."

Christy was appalled that Brandt could be so insubordinate to a captain. She knew the chain of command and obeyed it like the eleventh commandment: "Thou shalt not question those who rank above you." Brandt was either very secure in his popularity with the troops or stupid enough to undermine the leadership of a captain. The lieutenant seemed determined to self-destruct his career back down to sergeant.

Frustrated, Hillard turned to Christy. "Just go ahead and type both reports and notify me when they're done." He turned to Brandt. "Contact Razulo and find out what the hell he was doing in Area One at 0500 hours. If he indicates he was following leads on Lehman, strongly remind him that he's off that case from here on out. Tell him to go find another penny-ante drug dealer to bust. There's plenty around here to keep him busy."

"Done," Brandt said with a grin on his face. He gave a mock salute, motioned to his posse and they filed out the door.

"Insolent sonofabitch," Hillard muttered. He took the

cup of coffee discretely left on Christy's desk and sat on the metal edge as he blew on the hot brew.

Uncomfortable with being a witness to all the head-butting and now sharing her desk with the captain's tush, Christy kept silent. The captain would decide where and when the next words were spoken. He stayed silent for a long time, sipping his coffee, and looking into the blackness as if answers would magically appear in the steam.

"I really prefer tea," he said.

Caught off-guard by the unexpected remark, Christy said, "Me, too."

He looked at her as if seeing her as a person for the first time. "I like Constant Comment. The guys rib me about it."

"I like Irish Breakfast tea," Christy replied. She, too, felt the captain's choice of tea was, well, wussy.

"Irish Breakfast is a good tea," he agreed. "I don't care for green tea. I'm not sure what all the fuss is about."

"It's healthy." *Enough about tea, already.*

"Why does everything healthy have to taste like hell?" He sounded disconsolate.

Christy knew he wasn't talking tea anymore. "Sir, even if this hit-and-run is just some personal vendetta between locals, I think you're wise to look at the incident in broader strokes," she offered

Hillard contemplated her, making her shift uncomfortably. He took a sudden interest in straightening out the papers on her desk. "My men think I'm making too much of these deaths. They aren't verbalizing it, but I know they're glad some of the low-life's are being killed off. All of these victims have been repeat offenders, the troublemakers who make patrolling up here a pain. I'm sure some of the deputies wouldn't mind looking the other way because of all the senseless crime these people commit." Hillard blushed, shamefaced to be unburdening himself to Christy. That didn't stop him from adding, "The sheriff wants the problem to go away. Election year is coming up. All he's worried about are stats."

Law enforcement was less about going by the book and more about producing the numbers. Stats could make or denigrate a unit. This unspoken rule pressured everyone into finding ways to close cases, sometimes too hastily. That's where lawyers came in handy. Convictions were part of *their* stats.

Christy felt sorry for the guy. He was trying to do a good job but losing the respect of his men in the process. Upstaged by the obviously popular lieutenant, eclipsed by Brandt's charisma, Hillard was losing his grip on his authority. Christy realized he was caught in the middle of a power play by an underling and pressure from a politically ambitious sheriff. She was glad she wasn't in his shoes.

Draining his cup of the now-cold coffee, Hillard sighed and stood up. "It's been good talking to you," he said awkwardly. He stuck out his hand.

Surprised at the unexpected and respectful handshake, Christy responded to his firm grip. As he opened the door to leave, Hillard turned around. "I'm sorry if we've treated you less than hospitably. I really do appreciate the work you do. I know you weren't given a choice for this job, but I think you're the right person for the work. You've been efficient and you've put up with all the crap the men have thrown at you. I'm going to put a commendation in your personnel jacket."

Not that his praise would get her a pay raise or promotion, but the gesture was appreciated.

CHAPTER 23

By the time Brent came to pick her up, Christy was exhausted. The reports were graphic and the hit-and-run was gruesome. There were no skid marks. Study of the tire tracks on the legs of the victim showed that Slepski wasn't killed on the first attempt. He managed to crawl several feet away before the tire treads indicated the vehicle backed over him, as if the driver wanted to make sure he'd done the job right. This action erased all doubts that the initial contact might be accidental. Finally, deep treads on the torso of the body revealed that the driver took his time going forward, perhaps even stopping to let the full weight of the vehicle crush Slepski into road kill.

"Tough day?" Brent asked as he watched Christy

drag herself out of the chair, unplug the coffee pot, and pick up her purse.

"Nasty hit-and-run," she replied.

"Oh yeah, that's all everyone's talking about in town. The guy wasn't too popular."

Christy glared at him.

"Hey, I'm just relaying what I've been hearing all day." Brent put his hands up in defense. "Don't kill the messenger. At least, not until you I show you your surprise."

He held the door open and waited for her response. Sitting on the gravel was her midnight blue Saturn. Sunshine gleamed off the highly polished hood.

Christy ran forward, wanting to embrace her car despite the hot metal. "How did you get it out of impound?"

"I arm wrestled the guard." Brent dangled her car keys. Jingling alongside the car and house keys was a small frame and a photo of Shamus. "Good thing I won or he would have sold your car for scrap."

Christy grabbed the keys as Brent held the door open. He climbed in on the passenger side.

"Where's your Jeep?" she asked as she contentedly listened to the familiar hum of the motor.

"I took it in for some repairs. Maintenance. Trucks take a beating on these roads."

Christy wasn't listening. Brent had even cleaned the inside of the car. Somehow, the new car smell was back. *They have a spray for this?* she thought.

Christy turned to him and felt stupid tears welling up. "You did all this for me?"

"You deserve to be treated special," he said. "Down to the last detailing."

Christy pulled out of the driveway, deliberately taking her time to relish being behind the wheel at last.

"We'll never get home at this rate." Brent laughed. "The speed limit is over 15 miles an hour."

Christy ignored him. All the deprivation she'd felt from the beginning of the week was ebbing. With her car back came freedom and even trust. No, she wouldn't take leg bail down the foothills to the flatland. She was invested in the case. She wanted to support Hillard and repay his trust. Now she could appreciate the beauty of her surroundings and take an interest in the town and the people. Brent made for a nice diversion, certainly an added attraction and a terrific roommate.

When they got back to the cabin, Brent had T-bones marinating in the refrigerator, Diet Dr Pepper on ice and pasta salad. There was no deli around, so Christy had to assume the man knew how to boil water in addition to his many other accomplishments. All that was required of her was to unwind and de-stress.

Since the evening was mild, they decided to dine al fresco. Christy set places at a small redwood picnic table, away from the barbecue smoke. She liked her steak medium rare, blood running. He liked his medium well. Both were cooked to perfection. Brent's skill at the grill went undisputed. The pasta salad had a rich tang from Muscat Champagne Vinaigrette. She'd seen the bottle in the refrigerator and knew it wasn't an item from Hobbs Market. All the country store would carry would be cider vinegar. Artichoke hearts and pieces of pimento made a colorful confetti.

When they'd finished off every scrap of meat from the bone, Brent stood up and announced, "I've got a surprise." He slipped his hands into oven mitts and pulled off the grill. He went into the cabin and came out with a bag of marshmallows and two long pieces of wire.

"We're going to toast marshmallows!"

The child came out in both of them as they speared the marshmallows three deep on the wires then slowly turned them to brown on all sides. Greed and impatience caused several to char or melt through and drop on the coals. They "toasted" each other and Brent wiped sticky residue off her chin with his thumb.

"Sugar rush," Christy finally declared and put her spear down in defeat.

"I know a great cure." He guided her back to the redwood table, had her straddle the bench, and began kneading her shoulders.

"And he gives massages as well as cooks," Christy said as her head lolled back.

"I'm the whole package."

Yes, you are. Aloud, she said, "There's only one thing that would make this evening perfect."

"What's that?"

"A bubble bath." She sighed. "Your shower's fine, but I really miss my claw-footed bathtub back at my apartment."

"I'll bet you take long soaks with a book and a glass of Dr Pepper." His strong fingers followed the rhythm of his words.

"I drive my roommate nuts," she confessed. "We only have one bathroom."

Home seemed remote under Brent's mesmerizing strokes and hypnotizing voice. "What if I could give you what you wanted?" he asked.

"I think you are." Christy leaned back into the pressure.

He pushed her to an upright position. "Wait right here."

Her masseur took off and headed for a little shed on the side of the house. Pouting wasn't an option.

Brent returned carrying a galvanized tub. Although lightweight, it was large and oval-shaped. Maybe a horse trough or a cooler for a beer bash? He set the tub down in the middle of the room. The ranger then filled the spaghetti pot and every other pot in the cabin with water and set them to boiling on the stove.

"Is that a bathtub?" Christy asked as his actions began to make sense.

"It will be." Brent laughed. "Help me fill it."

They turned on the shower and together filled the tub

with hot water until there was no more left in the heater. Balancing the weight between them and sloshing water with every step, they placed the make-do bathtub in the middle of the room.

"Got any bubble bath?" Brent asked.

"Never leave home without it." Christy went to her cosmetic case and pulled out a small gift-size bottle of vanilla-fig scented shower gel, a gift from Christmas. She poured half of the contents and they motor-boated the water until suds appeared. An intoxicating sweetness filled the room.

"Your bath awaits you, m'lady."

Christy flicked bubbles into his face. Momentarily caught off-guard, Brent took a handful of suds and play-fully threw them on her hair. She shook her head and bubbles scattered like dust moats.

Boiling pots of water were added. With Brent stand-ing over her, Christy swirled the hot water into the bath until the temperature was perfect.

"I'll let you have some privacy," he said, suddenly embarrassed. "We're out of your favorite beverage so I'll make a Dr Pepper run."

Once she heard his car pull out, Christy slipped off her clothes, poured the rest of the wine into a glass, and slipped into the tub. The tin sides weren't as solid as the claw-footed tub at home and her knees stuck up as she tried to fit into the tight space, but it would do. She'd missed the sensation of being enveloped in hot water.

Pretending to be a woman of the Wild West in a boarding house tub, she slathered bubbles on her arms and breasts, breathing in the figgy scent.

A car crunched the gravel. *He's back so soon.* Christy knew Brent was too much of a gentleman to barge in. None of his actions indicated this was a ploy to catch her naked. That's why she was unprepared when the door opened.

Rod stood in the entry, armed with flowers and a silly grin on his face.

"What the hell are you doing here?" Christy screamed as she grabbed for the towel.

"Good to see you too," he replied.

Before the conversation could go further, a voice shouted "Hands up!"

Flowers scattered to the floor as Rod went for his weapon.

"Don't," Brent commanded. He shoved the shotgun into the intruder's back to make his point.

CHAPTER 24

Christy, what's going on?"

Their voices worked in unison. Christy looked from lover to roommate.

She sat in tepid water, a towel barely covering her upper body, bubbles clouding her lower parts but dissolving fast.

The men were like statues, one frozen with his hand on his sidearm, the other poised with his rifle. The barrel lethally connected the two.

"I'm taking a bath," Christy said, pointing out the obvious. "I was enjoying myself until you two barged in."

"Who's this guy?" Rodrigo demanded.

"I'm the guy who lives here. Who the hell are you?"

Brent replied, giving Rod a poke with the gun barrel to emphasize his point.

"Rod, Brent. Brent, Rod. Now that you've been properly introduced could you tuck away the guns and turn your backs so I can get out of the tub?"

"I don't have to turn away. I've seen you naked before." The barrel was gone from his back and he turned to look at Brent. "You need to leave."

"This is my cabin," Brent said stubbornly.

"I'm standing up now. This is me standing up." Christy rose from the bath, Venus with a towel dripping water and clinging wetly to her thighs. She held the dry end firmly to her breasts.

Seeing two grown, armed men reduced to blushing boys by her near nudity seemed both ridiculous and empowering to Christy.

"Assuming we can be adults at this point, why don't you guys step outside and let me get dressed?" she suggested.

The idea was met with mumbling and grumbling, neither man wanting to give up his "protection" of the endangered female in their midst.

"Out!" she ordered.

They fled through the doorway.

Once she was dressed, she opened the door. Only Rodrigo was waiting.

"Where's Brent? You didn't bury him in the woods, did you?"

Rodrigo barged past her, a stormy look on his dark features. He paced the floor, casing the cabin, doing his eagle-eye assessment of the scene, looking for clues. He was in full undercover mode, Christy noted, seeing him in action for the second time in her life. She let him process the information in any way he saw fit and waited until the Q and A began.

"You owe me an explanation," he finally said.

"You owe me one, too," she countered. "Let's start with what are you doing up here?" Christy walked past him and started picking up the flowers spread on the floor. Gerber daisies, Tiger Lily, white carnations, greenery, and baby's breathe. Some were worse for wear having been stepped on. She found a large cup, filled it with water and shoved in the stems. Flower arranging would come later.

"I called the apartment and Maxie told me you were on assignment up here," Rod said. He slumped down on the chair, his arms defensively crossed.

Christy went to the refrigerator and got a beer. She popped it open and handed the beverage to Rod. Always the perfect hostess.

Rod nodded and took a deep swallow. "I spotted Jim Wolfe at the substation and he gave me directions to the cabin."

I'll bet he enjoyed setting me up. Christy nodded, indicating that Rod should continue the narrative.

"I stopped by in town and picked up some flowers at

the little grocery store. I ran into Lennie and asked why you weren't staying with her, but she didn't want to talk to me for some reason." Rod took another chug. "I came here to surprise you and instead I find you shacking up with a forest ranger and naked in a tub. I think I deserve an explanation. That's where I'm at right now. Your turn."

Despite his deadly calm delivery, Rod was more angry than Christy had ever seen him. Having never been on the receiving end of his temper, she had no idea how far the black mood would go. Jealousy was not a trait she'd ever seen in Rod, but then, she'd never given Rodrigo anything to be jealous about.

"What was I supposed to do?" she replied. "The sheriff assigned me to the homicide team and put me here for the duration."

"They made you live with a strange guy? I can't believe the department would go that far."

"He wasn't here. We were borrowing his cabin. When the fires down south were over, he showed up." Christy spread her hands in frustration. "What was I supposed to do—kick him out of his own place?"

"You could have stayed with Lennie."

Christy closed her eyes and took a ragged breath. "We had a fight. We're not friends anymore."

Rodrigo downed that info with another swig of beer. "That's not possible. She's your best friend."

"My best friend has become a doormat for a worthless boyfriend. Plus, the detectives don't want me in contact with her because she owns the newspaper. They don't trust her anymore."

"Why didn't you insist the department put you in a hotel? You have rights."

"Have you seen the local accommodations?" Christy rolled her eyes. "I spent one night there and felt filthy. Plus, the county doesn't have money to spend. We're not the Feds."

Rod nodded. The Drug Enforcement Agency operated with a lot more lead way and sufficient funds in the field even with a tight economy.

"Plus, you're wrong," Christy continued. "I found out I didn't have rights. Nobody would listen to me, nobody cared how I lived as long as I was here to type up reports and handle the phones."

Rod shook the beer can. Empty. He crushed the metal. "I'm not happy with this situation."

"You're not happy?" Christy fired back. "You weren't even supposed to find out. I figured the case would be closed by now and I'd be home, just as you expected."

"So, this was a big secret?" Rod got up and took the can to the counter. "I came to you with flowers, looking forward to a romantic night in the woods, hoping you'd be as glad to see me as I was to be here. Instead, you're all defensive and acting pretty guilty."

"Are you accusing me of something?"

"Are you telling me nothing happened between you and this guy?"

Something had happened, Christy realized. She'd never told Brent she had a boyfriend. At the time, it simply didn't seem relevant, but now she wondered if she left out that detail because she wanted to keep her options open. She was always amazed a man as handsome and intelligent as Rodrigo was at her side, but the sensation of attracting an equally gorgeous and well-read man went to her head. Never before had two men vied for her affection.

"I like him," Christy finally admitted. "He's a gentleman. Nothing improper has happened."

"Except a romantic dinner." The remains of the meal and empty wine glasses were evidence.

"He cooks," Christy confessed. "I had a rough day at the office."

"And he thought he'd treat you to a bubble bath. We both know how a long soak puts you in a good mood."

Anger was unstoppable. "What is this? All of a sudden you've turned into a jealous Latin lover?" Christy fired with both barrels. "Yes, Brent happens to be an attractive man. He doesn't run off to other countries to fight a losing war on drugs. He fights fires and saves trees. He's an environmentalist, into the beauty of life, not the ugliness. He's opened me up to nature, taken away my fear of the great outdoors, and given me a little bit of inner peace. I need that right now." She realized she was verbalizing thoughts she'd been accumulating for the past few days. The words continued to tumble out, even though she knew they must sound like she was criticizing her lover. "He asks me how my day went instead of always being the one with exciting stories to tell. He listens. Not only that, but we have intense conversations. He reads Thoreau."

Rod stared at her. "I didn't give you those things? I didn't listen? I didn't hold you close when you were afraid of your own shadow? Tell me where I failed."

"No," Christy said, confused. "I mean yes, you did all that. But you aren't here. I need someone with me now. I've lost Lennie, I can't go home, there's a homicidal maniac running loose, and I need someone here. I needed a bath and Brent knew. He's given me exactly what I needed to get through today."

Rod looked down at the ground. "Fine. I'm glad you're okay. I won't worry about you anymore. I made a mistake coming up here and interfering with your job. I hope your detectives catch the killer and you get back to Coronita soon. Shamus misses you." He turned to leave.

"Rod, wait." Christy followed him out to the car. "I'm sorry this happened between us. It's awkward and we'll laugh about the whole mess later. But right now I just have a lot to deal with and Brent hanging out in his own place is just a minor inconvenience. For both of us. Nothing has happened and nothing will."

Rod opened the truck door and turned. "You're

wrong. Something has happened. You just haven't realized it yet. Brent is attracted to you. He's got an advantage over me because he's someone who can be here. He has time to get all zen with you. Go for it—write poetry, commune with nature, sit by the fire, and get literary. You knew who I was and what I did for a living before we got involved. Don't throw my career in my face. You don't have the right, after everything we've gone through."

Christy stood and watched the red tail lights and her relationship disappear down the road.

CHAPTER 25

When Brent showed up, Christy had already cried herself out and was sitting in bed with the comforter wrapped around her body. Without a word, he went to the woodpile and added a few thick branches to the stove.

"Are you all right?" he asked quietly.

"No, I'm not. My world just fell apart."

"Maybe it was built on a shaky foundation." He stirred the embers until the dry wood caught.

Christy shot him a scathing look. "Everything was fine before I came to Burlap."

Brent went over to her and cautiously sat on the edge of the bed. "Sometimes you reach a place where you're high enough to see your problems."

The Zen of Brent. His laid-back philosophy that seemed so attractive now rubbed like sandpaper.

"Your boyfriend has quite a temper," he remarked.

"I've never seen it before today," she replied.

"You've never made him angry before?"

Christy sighed. "We've never been together long enough to get on each other's nerves." She explained to Brent how Rodrigo's job with the Drug Enforcement Agency kept him on the move. "I'm like home base for him," she concluded.

"His North Star. You keep him pointed in the right direction." He gently cupped Christy's chin in his hand and tipped her head until she had to look into his eyes. "You're his lodestone."

She didn't know what that was exactly, but it sounded beautiful. Eloquent. God, did he have to be so poetic right now?

Christy could feel herself being lured in by the imagery he created. She was being seduced with words.

Rod was right. The man was downright dangerous.

Brent got up and fetched Thoreau from the bookshelf. "I want to read you something." He sat down and flipped through the well-worn book until he found the passage. "A wise man will know what game to play today, and play it. We must not be governed by rigid rules, as by the almanac, but let the seasons rule us." He paused to give her a meaningful look and took a deep breath before continuing. "The rules and thoughts of man are revolving just as steadily and incessantly as nature's. Nothing must be postponed."

That's when he kissed her. The book fell to the floor as Christy wrapped her arms around him and pulled him down on top of her.

CHAPTER 26

Christy lay in bed, the feel of a stranger's arm possessively cuddling her, wondering why she didn't feel more guilty.

When she felt Brent move and heard him yawn, remorse hit like a sledgehammer.

She quickly got up, grabbed her robe, and sprinted for the bathroom. Her hands shook as she put in her contacts.

Everything came into focus, including her behavior.

I've totally screwed up.

She shivered. The bathroom was icy. Christy turned the shower faucet full blast and prayed for hot water.

"Do you want me to join you?" Brent called through the door.

"No," she shouted back a little too emphatically. "Not this time," she amended.

What was she supposed to do now? She couldn't hole up in the bathroom for the rest of the day. As she stepped into the shower, she tried to think of excuses. A weak moment. Poetic words. Uncontrollable urges. Romantic firelight. Lack of common sense. Pick one.

"Christy, are you okay in there?"

Reluctantly, she turned off the water. *What happens now? How do I act normal?*

Brent was waiting for her when she opened the door. He went for a morning kiss, but she turned her head. "I didn't brush yet."

He laughed. "I hope you saved me some hot water." As he went around her, he called over his shoulder, "Coffee is just about done."

Tempting, but all Christy wanted to do was get dressed and leave the cabin.

No time to put on makeup.

She shoved a few basics into her purse and was nearly out the door when Brent came out of the bathroom with a toothbrush in his mouth.

"No breakfast? You haven't even had coffee." He took the toothbrush out and looked at her quizzically.

"Uh, no. I'll grab some at work. But, thanks for making it." *Do I kiss him goodbye? Are we at that stage already?*

"Okay. I guess I'll see you tonight." He didn't make

a move toward her, just casually turned to spit into the sink.

Christy climbed into her car, relieved to be out of his proximity.

It took all of her concentration to drive to the office. No other cars were in the lot because it was only 7 o'clock. She let herself in and immediately turned on the heat and the Mr. Coffee. Maybe she would stop shaking once she warmed up.

Facing herself in the mirror, make-up in hand, Christy realized the damage she'd done. It showed all over her face. Circles under the eyes from lack of sleep, lips raw from too many kisses. Oh yeah, and let's not forget a backache from falling off the bed. Where was that euphoric high she'd experienced last night?

"Nice going," she scolded herself.

In the bathroom, she pulled out concealer and went to work lightening up the dark circles under her eyes. A bit of face powder, blush—or not. Her face would turn plenty red if the guys sensed a sexual encounter—tinted Chapstick for her roughened lips, mascara. All the makeup tricks Lennie taught her.

Lennie. Christy looked at herself in the mirror. She wanted Lennie. Her friend was the only one she trusted, someone in whom she could confide her remorse. Lots of remorse to go around these days. Being judgmental about Lennie's relationship and life choices, remorse about the fight with Rod, turning too easily to the comfort of another man. Lennie wouldn't judge her back. Okay, there would be a bit of scolding, certainly a jab of humor at Christy's expense. Lennie was more cavalier about life and human weakness. These were traits Christy secretly sneered at in her friend. Now that she'd slipped off her own pedestal, Christy wanted the kind of forgiveness and perspective only Lennie could give.

It would take a phone call and some groveling, a good gulp of pride. But it was too early in the morning for confessions and pardons.

The detectives began trickling in, tired and prickly. The case wasn't going anywhere and leads were dying out faster than bodies. Pressure from Headquarters increased as *Kearny Sun* reporters took potshots at the investigation.

Apparently, this week the newspaper decided to back off from constant criticism of the local police department in order to point out the defects of the sheriff's department.

Burlap had gone from under the radar to headline news.

Wolfe waltzed in last. "Get your stuff," he ordered Christy. "We're going on a little road trip."

"Back to civilization?"

He grinned maliciously. "You wish. No, I'm going to show you a site you haven't seen in the wonderful burg of Burlap." He nodded to Deputy Espinoza and added, "It's been approved."

Reluctantly, Christy climbed into Wolfe's patrol car. He took the roads at warp speed, partially because he knew she hated his driving, probably because he could break speed laws with impunity. She hung on, refusing to give him the satisfaction of seeing her fear.

They came to a bridge crossing over the Kings River. The water was high and current fast with spring run-off. The Sierra Nevadas had been bare this year. Skiers were disappointed, but no more so than the farmers who waited each year to see how much water they could count on for their crops.

On the other side of the bridge was a guardhouse. Next to it was a sign announcing the site "Miramonte CDC." A man in the tan and olive green uniform of a correctional officer came out, recognized Wolfe, and waved them on.

"What is this place?" Christy asked, looking around at the long, one-story buildings made of concrete blocks.

"It's a prison camp."

Christy turned her head from side to side. "Where's the barbed wire?"

"Don't need it." He let that sink in before continuing. "This is a jail extension for exemplary prisoners. They come out here and train to fight fires. Pretty sweet way to serve time for a crime." Wolfe pointed to a solitary trailer on a hill. "That's for conjugal visits. Every jailbird wants to be assigned here."

Wolfe pulled to a halt and indicated she should get

out of the car. Men stopped what they were doing to stare. No wolf whistles, just curious appraisal. Wolfe seemed to be enjoying her discomfort as they walked to the command center.

"Hey, Smokey," Wolfe said, shaking the hand of a burly man. The name on the uniform pocket said "De Barr."

"You brought company," growled De Barr.

"This is office assistant Christy Bristol. She's assigned to type up investigation reports."

De Barr grunted his acknowledgment and indicated with a nod that they should sit down in the heavy wooden chairs in front of his desk.

"Coffee?" he asked. Without waiting for a response, he bellowed, "Cruz!"

A prisoner briskly entered the office and stood at attention.

"Coffee." De Barr paused and asked Christy in a much more gentle tone, "Will that be with cream and sugar, ma'am?"

"Yes. Thank you." Finally, a gentleman in the room.

"I take mine black," Wolfe injected.

"I don't care how you like it," De Barr drawled. "I'm not sure I want to waste coffee on you until you tell me why you're here."

Ticked, Wolfe got right to the point. "We heard you had an inmate go missing."

De Barr grunted, which Christy took as a yes.

"You might have heard of the murders happening in Burlap recently." There was a sarcastic tone in Wolfe's voice.

The big man leaned back in his chair causing it to groan. "I heard."

"I'd like to see his records."

De Barr looked at Wolfe as if he were an unwanted rodent with hantavirus. "We don't keep murderers up here. Non-violent criminals only."

"Maybe he went rogue."

"Or maybe he took off to see a giant Sequoia."

Christy watched as the two men stared each other down. Another alpha male pissing contest.

Wolfe refused to be beaten. Christy wondered if some of his posturing was for her benefit. Was she supposed to say "You da man!" to bolster his ego? *Why am I even here*? she wondered.

"Your inmates think this is a vacation spot? A chance to spend a little time in the National Forest, fresh air, good food, all on the taxpayers' dollars? Sounds like you're running a camp for wayward boys."

The commander cannonballed out of his chair, his massive arms bracing his bulk on the desk. "My men fight fires, build rock walls, dig water culverts, you little—" He stopped himself short of profanity, acknowledging Christy's presence.

She shrugged to let him know she agreed with his foul opinion of her ex-boyfriend.

"The 80 men up here work their butts off. We save the state of California 1.8 million dollars annually. That's a helluva lot more than your contribution to society, *Deputy* Wolfe."

Having raised hackles, Wolfe relaxed back in his chair with a smug grin on his face. "So, you're sure this escapee had nothing to do with the murder? Can I relay that message to the captain?"

"You can take it to the bank. The inmate was accounted for when those murders happened." De Barr glowered as he eased himself back into his padded chair. "Any more questions? I've got real work to take care of."

"What about your guards? Anybody got a beef with the lowlifes who are getting knocked off? You got a vigilante on your staff?"

"Get out." The command came out as a rumble with a threat behind it.

Wolfe stood up and Christy followed his lead. "You will keep us informed of the prisoner's status, right, Commander? We'll want to question him when—or if—you locate him."

Before De Barr could come around to kick Wolfe's ass out the door, an officer opened it and announced, "They want the deputy back at the substation ASAP. There's been another murder."

"Looks like we have a suspect now, doesn't it, Commander?"

With that final volley, Wolfe sauntered out the door. Christy followed.

Once on the gravel of the yard, he grabbed her arm and rushed them both to the patrol car.

CHAPTER 27

Once in the vehicle, Wolfe grabbed his radio. Dispatch gave him the location and he took off, spitting gravel in his wake.

"Aren't you going to drop me off at the office?" Christy asked when she saw they were headed in the opposite direction.

"No time. We're close to the crime scene so we're going to see what they've got."

Again, a roller coaster ride through the hills, this time with the siren echoing off the rock outcroppings. Christy could feel waves of nausea coming on with every twist of the steering wheel.

Telling Wolfe to slow down wouldn't do any good.

She took deep breaths and tried to focus on the dashboard, hoping the journey would be short. They came around the corner and nearly hit Deputy Espinoza in the middle of the road directing traffic. Four cars were already at the scene: two other patrol cars, an undercover vehicle, and an old Volkswagen bus with faded peace symbols and the portrait of the Zig-Zag man painted on the side.

Everyone was standing around one of the weird cement sculptures that dotted the area. This one was blue. The abstract piece of "art" resembled a building block with two small square holes on the bottom and one large U-shaped hole at the top. The bottom of the U was about a foot wide and flopped over it was a body.

Christy would have preferred to stay in the car, but Wolfe motioned her to get out "You're part of the team now. Act like it."

From the perimeter of the group, Christy could see the victim was a Hispanic man. So far, this was the first Hispanic she'd seen in Burlap, other than men at the prison yard. It dawned on her that this might be the missing inmate.

She was wrong.

"Naw, the escapee was Caucasian," Lieutenant Brandt was saying to the detective who came to the same conclusion. "We think this guy is from a marijuana grow. It's planting season. Locals have been finding supply drop-offs of propane, beans, and tortillas near the road leading to the National Forest."

Nobody touched the body as they waited for Ann Pulido to come up the hill with the forensic van. Instead, they cracked nervous jokes about rigor mortis making the corpse as hard as the cement it was lying on. Somebody tagged the victim a "stoner." That brought snickers from everyone except the long-haired owner of the van who twitched nervously in the company of cops.

The sun was beating down on the unshaded area. Everyone was getting antsy in the heat.

They turned in unison at the clip-clopping sound of horse hoofs. Around the corner rode a woman on horseback. She carried a leather pouch with the words "U.S. Postal Service" etched on the side.

She reined in the horse and sat erect, taking in the scene. A single black braid hanging over one shoulder from under a baseball cap and her earthy complexion indicated Native American heritage. The stony expression on her face registered no surprise at the cluster of deputies or the corpse hanging from the sculpture. Just another day on her route. With a shrug, her booted heels flicked the stirrups and her mount stoically continued down the road. There was an eerie silence from the group. Nobody attempted to run after her and bring her back for questioning.

Breaking the mood, Lieutenant Brandt barked, "Espinoza! Drive over to Hobbs Market and pick up some sodas. You." He pointed at Christy. "Are all the reports typed up at the office?"

"Yes, sir."

He looked her up and down. "Then take the rest of the afternoon off," he said magnanimously.

Relieved, Christy climbed into the patrol car with Espinoza. He didn't say much as he steered down the road and into Burlap.

As they passed the *Burlap Bag* office, Christy saw Lennie's Land Rover parked in front of the trailer. "Why don't you let me out here?" Christy suggested.

"Isn't your car back at the substation?"

She waved the deputy away. "I'll pick it up later."

It was time to break the ice and repair the damaged friendship.

CHAPTER 28

Christy started to knock on the door, but then remembered this wasn't just Lennie's residence, but the community newspaper office. She let herself in. A small bell jingled as she closed the door.

"Be right there," Lennie's voice echoed down the hall.

When she turned the corner and saw Christy, she stopped.

"Can we talk?" Christy asked plaintively.

"I sure think it's about time, don't you?" Lennie came the rest of the way down the hall and grabbed her in a bear hug. "Don't you ever ignore me like that again."

"I was being stupid," Christy said.

"And I was being snotty," Lennie countered. She

propelled Christy into the kitchen and sat her down at the table. "I just happen to have a cold one waiting for you." She opened the fridge and pulled out a Diet Dr Pepper for Christy and a beer for herself.

After a few gulps of soda, Christy got control of herself. The reunion was going easier than expected. "Is Jacob around?" she asked.

"He heard on the scanner there was another murder victim and he and Linda went racing out of here. We've got the place to ourselves."

"I just came from the scene. The body's hanging on one of those weird sculptures." She took another swallow. "Linda's going to get a great photo for the front page."

Lennie looked at her with surprise. "They let you go out on crime scenes now? That's a step up."

Christy gave a wry laugh. "Hardly. Wolfe decided to give me a field trip out to the CDC. We were there when the call came in. The lieutenant gave me the day off while they collect evidence and make reports." She sighed. "I needed the break. I've done so much typing the last couple of days, I'll probably get carpal tunnel."

"Not the vacation you were expecting, I guess."

Confession time. "Lennie, I really messed up."

Lennie reached across the table and put her hand over Christy's. "It's okay. We both said things we didn't mean. Water under the bridge."

"No, I mean I really messed up." She had trouble

looking her friend in the eyes. "I'm staying in the cabin of a forest ranger—"

"I heard about that."

"—and he came back from fighting a forest fire down south."

Lennie's eyebrows rose. "I didn't hear that news flash."

"Then Rodrigo showed up and—"

"Whoa," Lennie interrupted. "Back up. If you're in the cabin and Mr. Ranger is in the cabin, what are the sleeping arrangements?"

"It was his place, Lennie. I couldn't throw him out of his own home." Christy could hear the defensiveness in her voice.

Lennie shook her head. "This story doesn't sound like it has a happy ending."

"Rodrigo caught me taking a bath—"

"With the ranger?"

"No!" Christy protested. "Brent was getting wood for more hot water."

Lennie took a swig of beer. She seemed to be enjoying the story. "Cozy. So what did Rod do?"

"He got really pissed off at me. We had a fight and he took off."

Lennie leaned back in the chair and shrugged. "Okay. You had a fight. There's a lot of that going around these days. When you get done with the investigation, you go back to Coronita and have make-up sex.

That's the game plan. It's all good."

"Easy for you to say," Christy countered.

She saw Lennie scrutinize her with that narrow-eyed squint she used when she sensed a cover-up. Nothing got past Lennie.

"What aren't you telling me?"

Christy took a deep breath. "I slept with him, Lennie. I slept with Brent."

Confession wasn't good for the soul at all. She felt ashamed to admit she'd been unfaithful, especially to Lennie. Not that Lennie was a paragon of fidelity. Christy always felt her friend's promiscuity was a sign of weak character. But Christy also knew she was the one person she could count on not to be judgmental.

"How was it?"

Christy pulled herself out of self-loathing. "What?"

"This Brent guy. How was he in bed?"

Christy's became indignant. "Lennie, that's not the point. I was unfaithful to Rod."

Lennie shrugged. "Yeah, I get that. I'm just hoping the sex was worth the horse whipping your giving yourself."

Pure Lennie. "Okay, it was good," Christy reluctantly admitted. "Are you happy now?"

"I want details."

"I'm not giving you details," Christy snapped.

"I know you, girlfriend, and you aren't the type to just jump in bed at the drop of a guy's pants. That's my thing. So what made this man different?"

Good question. "You mean besides the cozy fire and the romantic dinner he cooked me? The fact that he listened to my problems and made the effort to give me a warm tub to soak in?"

"He would have had me with just dinner. But, you—you don't give it away that easy."

Christy got up and paced around the small kitchen. "I don't know, Lennie. He was different, you know? I mean, Rodrigo is fantastic, but Brent has a more romantic side. He loves nature, relates to the forest, he seems happy with so little. He reads Thoreau."

"Don't know who that is."

Christy knew Brent's literary leanings weren't going to rate high on Lennie's hot meter. "Thoreau was a man who went into the woods at Walden Pond and wrote about nature."

"Oh, you mean Doonsbury. I never understood that comic strip." Lennie waved her hand, dismissing her own cluelessness. "So the ranger is educated, romantic, and sexy. You were in the moment. Your hormones took over. That's all there was to it, right?"

Was it?

What she'd felt with Brent wasn't just sexual attraction. The man met her on an intellectual level, something she missed working in the machismo atmosphere of law enforcement.

Christy hadn't felt the void until Brent came along.

Stimulating conversations with him felt like foreplay. It certainly led to sex.

"Now, we gotta do damage control," Lennie announced. "Are you going to keep sleeping with the ranger?"

Christy registered shock. "No. I couldn't even face him this morning."

"You've got to face him sometime. I mean, you're living in his cabin."

Lennie was right. "I could ask Captain Hillard to put me back in the hotel."

"The sheriff already decided not to spend money to keep you happy," Lennie reminded her. "I think you have to go back to our original plan. Stay here with me."

"Jacob's not going to go along with that, Lennie."

"Things aren't going too well between us, anyway. All he does is brag about how this murder spree is going to get him a job with *The Kearny Sun.*" She shook her head. "He's actually happy that bodies are dropping like flies. The other day I heard him tell Linda he would have killed those low-lifes himself if he'd known it was his ticket out of here. He's so cold-hearted, I couldn't believe it."

"It's disturbing," Christy agreed. "There's not much sympathy for the victims. Even Brent called them 'the dregs of society.' I heard the detectives laughing that some civic-minded killer was just 'taking out the trash.' I know these aren't the most desirable people in the community, but I can't believe everyone is okay with what's going on." She shook her head. "I just want to get out of this insanity and go home."

"I'm fed up with it, too." Lennie looked across the table. "I miss Kearny and shopping at the mall, decent restaurants, and normal crimes. I want to drive my Jaguar and pick up hunky men at the health club. I gave this newspaper business and Jacob my best shot. Time to do something different for a change."

That's the Lennie I know. "We're flatlanders," Christy agreed.

"Flatlanders and proud of it."

So many decisions on empty stomachs. "I think we should celebrate," Lennie announced. She jumped up from the table and grabbed her purse. "I know just the place two girlfriends can drown their sorrows."

"Ronnie's Roadhouse?"

"Oh, better than that."

CHAPTER 29

Trudy's Sugar Shack resembled a gingerbread cottage with white scallop trim, pink window frames, and a bright pink door. Lawn ornaments that looked like an over-sized chocolate chip cookie, a strawberry ice cream cone, a candy cane, and a cupcake sprouted at the entrance. Christy half expected Hansel and Gretel to pop out and greet them.

Owner Trudy Meyers definitely did not look like a witch. She was tall, peach complected, had light brown hair, soft brown eyes, and no discernible warts. Her pink frilly apron was lightly dusted with flour.

"Good morning, ladies. Care for a sample?" she beamed as she held out a plate of brownies.

Lennie didn't hesitate. "My God, they're still warm,"

she said through a mouthful of crumbs. "Oh Christy, you have to try one. They're heavenly."

Lennie was right. They were a bit of dark chocolate heaven. Christy closed her eyes and let the cocoa take over. Tiny bits of shaved chocolate melted on her tongue. She never imagined a brownie could taste so exquisite.

Lennie licked her fingers and started casing the bakery case. "Oh, cheesecake. Boston cream pie. Look, she has napoleons."

"I have cream puffs, too." Trudy pointed to a tray on the far end. The puffs were filled with rich, creamy pudding. Dribbled on top were ribbons of chocolate.

"I can't choose, I really can't. Let's get one of each," Lennie decided.

Christy felt her adult side fighting her inner child. "That's too much pastry."

"We don't have to eat it all at once." Lennie had no rein on her sweet tooth. She was literally a kid in a candy store.

Trudy got the largest box she had and started filling it with two items from each offering before Lennie changed her mind. The box was nearly full when Lennie's head jerked up and her nose sniffed like a bloodhound.

"Do I smell banana bread?" she asked.

Trudy hesitated. "Yeah, I just took it out of the oven."

"That's my favorite. I'd like a loaf."

The request made Trudy uncomfortable. "I'm afraid it's a special request from one of my regulars."

But Lennie was not to be deflected that easily. "Just a few slices. Please. I can't leave without trying the banana bread," she pleaded.

Trudy sighed and went through the kitchen door. She came out with a wax-paper bag.

Carrying forty dollars' worth of goodies, the women made their way back to the trailer. Lennie made a pot of coffee while Christy put out a large platter and started unloading their bounty.

"Let's try the banana bread while it's still warm," Lennie suggested. She reached into the bag and pulled out a slice.

Christy waited until the coffee was ready and then took a slice. It was rich with the taste of bananas and a spice she had trouble recognizing. Cardamom? Definitely fresh nutmeg. A hint of ginger? Trudy probably had a secret mix she used so nobody could copy her unique flavors. The kitchen was warm and cozy with the smell of coffee accompanying every bite.

Lennie sighed. "I don't think I've ever tasted anything this good."

"We bought way too much," Christy admonished.

"Yeah, but how could we possibly choose?"

Christy picked up a petit four. "The bakery is just down the street. You could get a treat every day if you wanted."

"Not with Jacob counting my calories."

They both rolled their eyes and burst into laughter.

"I'll bet sugar wouldn't melt in his mouth," Christy said, trying to catch her breath.

"Even my sugar can't sweeten him up. And I'm just one big honeypot." Lennie licked cupcake icing off her finger seductively.

"Yes, you are," Christy agreed. She picked up a cream puff and stuck her tongue deep into the custard.

"Sexy!" Lennie grabbed the other cream puff, slowly licked the opening, then pressed her lips against the puff, and sucked in the cream.

"Are you getting it on with that cream puff?"

"I have an oral fixation," Lennie replied.

They both burst into a fit of laughter. Christy picked up a cupcake and offered it to her friend's mouth. Lennie stuck her tongue out and swirled it around the frosting then took the cherry in her teeth and winked.

Christy doubled over with glee. "I can't believe we're molesting pastries."

"You started it."

Christy looked at the plate of sweet concoctions in front of her. "We should stop. The sugar overload is going to be fatal."

Lennie nodded and sipped her coffee. She closed her eyes and inhaled the rich aroma. "I'm so glad I inherited Mt. Rainer Coffee. I mean, look at me. I went from having less than nothing to all this."

Christy looked around the office. "Well, you didn't get very far. I mean, you're still living in a trailer."

They both burst out laughing again.

Lennie belted out "Freedom. Freedom. Freedom!" and launched into her Aretha Franklin imitation.

"Think. Think what you're trying to do to me," they sang together.

They ran out of the right lyrics and stopped to catch their breath.

Finally settled down, Lennie's eyes caressed the remaining goodies. "You know, we really should finish them off. If Jacob comes home, he'll have a fit."

"Good point," agreed Christy as she grabbed for a napoleon.

"Funny, I don't feel the least bit full," Lennie said through crumbs of a black/white, walnut/chocolate chunk cookie.

"I'm fighting off guilt."

"That's the good Catholic in you."

Again, convulsions of laughter.

"Mea Culpa." Christy reached for another cupcake. "Bless me Father, for I have sinned." She crammed the top of the cake into her mouth.

"What's going on here?"

Jacob. Like guilty children instead of grown women, Lennie and Christy jerked around. Jacob was posed by the kitchen stove, hands on hips, ready to read them the riot act.

Christy looked at Lennie, who was trying hard to gulp down the rest of the cookie in her mouth. She choked.

Christy knew she had frosting circling her lips. Feeling clown-foolish, she reached for a napkin.

"You decided to make a pig of yourself, Lennie? Is that what this is all about?" He waved his arm over the banquet of pastries like they were poison.

"Want some?" Lennie coughed. She offered him a cookie. He smacked it out of her hand.

Too much drama. Without warning, Lennie went into a fit of laughter, nearly falling out of her chair. The tension broken, Christy crossed her arms on the table and rested her head on them like a pillow. She convulsed into giggles.

"Are you two stoned?" Jacob demanded.

"No." Lennie tried to get her eyes focused on him. "We're just having a good time. You remember what a good time feels like, right?"

Christy jerked her head up and tried to catch her breath. "You tell 'em, girlfriend. We got our cake and we're eating it, too."

Another wave of laughter washed over them. They held on to each other to keep from falling to the floor.

"You two disgust me." Jacob turned on his heel and stormed out of the trailer.

Calmer now, Lennie looked at Christy. "Do you think he's right?"

"You mean about being disgusting? No." Christy picked up a piece of banana bread. "But I think I know what the secret ingredient is in Trudy's banana bread."

CHAPTER 30

Christy crashed in Lennie's spare room, sleeping off the high from the sugar and possibly weed. When she woke up, she realized she had to get a fresh change of clothes at the cabin. Awkward. She knocked at the master bedroom door.

"Lennie, get up. You have to drive me to the cabin."

"Come on in. He's not here."

Christy cracked the door. Lennie was sprawled in bed, still groggy from the last night's revelry.

"Jacob didn't come home?"

"Apparently not." Lennie stretched and grabbed for a pair of jeans on the floor. She shoved them on under an over-sized sleep T-shirt. With a bit of fishing around under the bed, she came up with tennis shoes. "Ready."

ᗋᕝᕗ

Now it was Christy's turn to face her indiscretions. As they turned into the dirt pathway to the cabin, she was relieved to see the Jeep missing. Maybe he'd already left for the day.

"Come on in, I'll only be a minute."

Lennie entered the cabin and her eyes swept the small space. "Cozy." She bounced on the small bed. "Very cozy. I can see how hard it would be to resist temptation. Close quarters and all."

Christy was about to say something about rubbing it in when she spotted a note on the counter.

> *Dear Christy,*
> *Sorry about Rod. Away LA area, big fire.*
> *See you in a few days.*
> *XXOO*

"I'm off the hook for now." She showed the note to Lennie.

"Double hugs and kisses. Nice touch. This guy's a keeper." Lennie tossed the note back on the counter. "Looks like you've got a few days lead time to come up with a solution."

"Maybe they'll arrest a killer and I won't have to make any decisions."

The women looked at each other, knowing neither of

them would be let off that easily. Christy hurriedly changed into fresh underwear and a clean top. She grabbed necessary make-up, deodorant, and the blow dryer from the bathroom. With any luck, the guys wouldn't be at the office yet and she could pull herself together. Right now, she looked like hell.

"What about the rest of your stuff?" Lennie looked around the cabin as Christy was heading for the door.

"We can figure that out after work. I don't think Jacob is going to want me at your place."

"Right now, I don't want Jacob at my place either."

Lennie dropped Christy off at the substation. The Saturn was the lone car in the parking lot. Christy unlocked the door, grateful that none of the detectives, especially Wolfe, could witness her entrance. What was it they called it on *Sex and the City*? The "walk of shame?"

She put on a pot of coffee and ducked into the bathroom to do damage control. Using her fingers to run water through her bangs, she used the blow dryer to freshen them up. For the rest, she bent over and brushed her hair toward the ground, then flipped her head up so the hair looked full and freshly washed. Sort of. Once her contacts were in, she slapped on a bit of lilac eye shadow and plum liner. Her eyes were oddly red and there were dark circles under them, now hidden by a bit of concealer. A touch of gloss was as much as she could muster before grabbing a hot cup of badly needed coffee.

Instead of sitting down and getting right to work,

Christy lingered by the doorway and looked out over the trees glittering with morning dew. All morning she'd felt like she was on a race course, fearful to get her clothes from the cabin, worried about confronting Brent, rushing to get to work before her car was discovered still in the parking lot. Finally, a chance to breathe.

Christy felt the tug of residual guilt about ingesting illegal drugs, no matter that she broke the law unwittingly. *How ironic,* she thought. *Here I am at work, coming off a hellacious high. Good thing the department doesn't do drug testing.*

For a first-time drug experience, she had to admit, it really wasn't too bad. She remembered every bite of pastry; she closed her eyes and felt the texture of the cream, frosting, buttery flakes. Yeah, she was bloated today and her pants were snug. How had they devoured that much junk food in so short a time? Must be what stoners called "the munchies." Bits of conversation came back to her: things said that made sense at the time and seemed oh, so important. She couldn't remember much of the gabfest, but it seemed centered around making decisions on the men in their lives. What she did recall was laughing until her sides hurt. Everything was so darn funny!

Now she understood why people wanted to legalize marijuana. She's heard all the arguments that it was good medicine and a cash crop that could take California out of the weeds—economically speaking—but bottom line? It was fun. Christy couldn't remember the last time she'd giggled like a thirteen-year-old or gobbled sweet treats like a toddler.

She hadn't anticipated the paranoia that accompanied the high. When Jacob caught them in an orgy of sugar, the realization that she could be busted for drugs and lose her job, not to mention her spotless reputation, hit her hard. However fun the night had been, it wasn't worth the ultimate cost.

On the plus side, there was no hangover except red eyes, a few extra pounds, and the knowledge that she'd broken the law. What would Rod, who went to Mexico to apprehend drug dealers, say if he knew what she'd done?

She'd done a lot of things lately of which he wouldn't approve. Standing up for her right to conduct herself any way she wanted might have seemed like a good idea when she was wrapped in a bath towel. But Christy knew she'd put Rodrigo's trust in their relationship on the line. And, for what? A man who was only a temporary fixture in her life, no more than a fling, a flirtation. It felt good to flirt and, for the first time, she'd gotten the ego-rush of knowing another man found her attractive. How did beautiful women handle that kind of attention on a regular basis?

Faced with two options, she wondered if Brent was the better match for her? His love of nature, his literary bent, the fact that he stayed in the same country were all pluses. Both men had dangerous jobs, but at least Brent could freely talk about fighting fires. With Rodrigo, there would always be a curtain of secrets between them.

A patrol car pulled up and she saw Deputy Espinoza get out, holding a thick folder: her work for today, corrections in reports for her to enter into the computer.

"TGIF," he greeted her, handed off the paperwork, and headed right for the coffee. "I'll bet they keep us up here and make us work all weekend. That's going to thrill my wife. It's my daughter's third birthday."

Christy slid into her desk chair and let her hair veil her face, just in case there was some sign flashing "Stoner" over her features. Just her nagging conscience. Or, maybe it was Celeste sending reprimands her way. Nobody inflicted guilt better than a self-righteous nun.

When Wolfe came through the door, he barely acknowledged Christy.

"We've got some leads," he informed Espinoza. "All these murder victims are definitely connected by drugs. Marijuana is the primo crop for this area and they're growing it in the National Forest."

"So does that mean we have to work with the narcs?" Espinoza asked.

"Well, yeah—you got a problem with that?"

The deputy shrugged. "It's just that they're glory hounds. You know they're going to try to take all the credit for busting the case, not just busting a few pot growers."

"Careful," Wolfe warned. "I was one of those 'glory hounds' in the recent past. Isn't that right, Christy?"

"Yep." Her fingers flew over the keyboard as she feigned disinterest.

"For them it's just stats," insisted the deputy. "All they can do is pull plants out of the earth. That's not going to solve these cases."

"Look." Wolfe turned to his co-worker. "We all work for the sheriff. They don't have any training in homicide investigating. Don't worry about who gets the credit until we solve the murders, okay?"

The parking lot started filling up quickly as every member of the investigation, including the captain and lieutenant, converged on the substation. Any fears of being noticed subsided as Christy realized she was being treated like another piece of office furniture. They walked past her, talking heatedly, not even bothering to give her a nod.

The latest corpse injected detectives with new life and purpose. Christy realized the backwater case was accelerated to the top of the sheriff's list of priorities. Nervous sweat on Captain Hillard's face confirmed her suspicions.

Bodies swelled beyond the doors of the small conference room. As Espinoza suspected, the narcotics team was there, as well as vice and forensics. Everyone who was anyone in the Central County Sheriff's Department wanted a piece of the action.

The investigation had grown to task-force status. Vehicles overflowed the parking lot and down the hillside.

For the first time, Christy could hear what was going on in the inner sanctum—the proverbial fly on the wall. She slipped her headset on, even though there was no tape in the transcription machine, and pretended to type a report. If anyone glanced her way, they would assume she was deaf to the discussion.

Once Hillard called for order and voices subsided, the captain launched into an update for the newcomers. This was old news to Christy. The number of murders and their causes were outlined, the time line and locations noted.

No suspects were mentioned. The initial team was coming up dry on that count.

"There was no attempt on the part of the perpetrator to hide the latest victim," Hillard explained. "The body was left, not only in plain sight for us to find, but staged in a way that indicates the killer is becoming more blatant in his actions."

"He's rubbing our noses in it, that's what he's doing," chimed in Lieutenant Brandt. "He's making us look like idiots."

"What do we know about the killer?" a voice asked.

"Not much," Hillard admitted. "I'm not a profiler, but we can assume the suspect is male, probably in his late twenties to thirties, a local who knows the area, and, judging from the strength it would take to haul a body onto the cement sculpture where he was found, a large and strong individual."

"What about the hippie who found the body?" inquired another voice.

Brandt jumped in again. "Naw, we grilled the sucker at headquarters and, other than the fact that he smelled like weed and freaked out that we were gonna bust him for possession, it was just his bad luck to be the first on the scene."

"Is there anything that links the victims?" came the next question.

Christy listened intently. The same question was nagging her.

"Bottom-feeders." Brandt's voice interrupted before the captain could respond. "These men were the dregs of Burlap society. Drug dealers, burglars, drunks, all of them probably on welfare. Whoever's killing them is doing the county a favor."

"That's enough, Brandt." Hillard's temper finally exploded. "You will treat this case without prejudice. Understand?"

"Yes, sir," Brandt replied, no sign of respect in his voice.

He's undermining the captain, Christy realized. She wondered what that dynamic was all about. Insubordination in the ranks didn't fly with the department.

"We have established," the captain continued, "that all of the victims were in a low income bracket. They grew up in this area and, although they don't own property, they come from the original founders of Burlap. We're told by the locals that they have a feeling of entitlement to the land and a resentment of outsiders, especially people purchasing cabins on what they still consider their property."

"Sir." Espinoza, who was on the outskirts of the crowd, waved his hand in recognition. Christy watched as he moved his way farther into the room. "I've worked Area One for two years and all the victims are well known to patrol officers. Over my time here, I've personally arrested every one of them on a range of charges. They are all repeat offenders."

"That's correct, deputy. We have rap sheets on each of the men."

"Well, sir, the ones I arrested were all released from jail due to overcrowding. Maybe one or more victims of their criminal activity decided to take matters into their own hands."

A silence filled the room. Apparently, Espinoza had hit a nerve.

Hillard hurried to fill the void. "I'm not going to address the jail issue. That's a political hotbed between the sheriff and the board of supervisors. It has no place in this investigation."

"Does vigilantism have a place?" challenged Brandt.

"Let's not head in that direction, Lieutenant."

The standoff was on.

"With all due respect, *sir*," Brandt said, with absolutely no respect in his tone, "we're running around with our heads up our asses looking for suspects when there are a ton of possibilities living in this town. Everyone we've talked to has some sort of grudge against the homicide victims. Since we aren't effectively doing our jobs and letting felons out of jail, stands to reason one of the locals might decide to take matters into his own hands."

Christy heard a low grumble wash across the group.

"Has anything in the investigation showed evidence of this action?" Captain Hillard's voice was edgy.

"We haven't trained our focus on anyone except the obvious," was Brandt's comeback.

"Have you found any connection between the victims and an individual who might have been a target of their illegal activities?" the captain persisted.

"Why does it have to be just one killer?" someone piped up.

"Maybe a group in town worked together to take out the garbage," added a second voice.

The deputies were being swayed by Brandt's insubordination and now circled the captain like sharks in a pool. Christy sensed a lack of respect for their superior officer. Department politics at its backstabbing best.

Finally, Hillard's temper got the best of him.

"I will not entertain this suggestion," he said heatedly. "Once we go in that direction, this whole investigation falls apart. I've got Sheriff Nolan breathing down my neck to get these murders solved. He's got the tabloids sniffing around headquarters for a story and they'd like nothing more than for us to hand them a conspiracy theory. We will contain our information, conduct ourselves accordingly, and nobody talks to the press. Understood? Dismissed."

As the deputies filed out, Christy saw many had smirks on their faces. Obviously, they'd enjoyed front row seats to the sparring between the captain and the lieutenant. Patrol cars roared to life and Christy heard the grind of gravel as they jammed out of the parking lot.

The conference room door slammed shut. Several sergeants and Lieutenant Brandt remained inside with Hillard. Christy stopped faking transcription and took off the headset to listen.

"Tonight, the locals are having a town hall meeting at the Rugged Cross Church," Hillard informed them. "I will be attending to represent the sheriff's department and field questions. I want a homicide detective and one of your sergeants there with me. I'm authorizing overtime."

Overtime was the magic word. Even Brandt wanted in. "I'm free," he volunteered.

"I've had enough of your input for today, Lieutenant," Hillard snapped.

Before Christy could get out of the line of fire for a breath of fresh air, the door swung open. Red-faced and neck vein pulsing, the captain exited in a flurry.

The sergeants followed with their heads down.

Brandt wrapped up the rear. "Bet you got an earful,"

he said, stopping at her desk. "You keep your mouth shut, understood? No squealing to your girlfriend or your sergeant. Got it?" He punctuated his words by forming his fingers into a gun and pulling the trigger.

She got it.

CHAPTER 31

The end of the workday signaled decision time. Should she go back to the cabin, pack her things, and move back to Lennie's or take a chance of Brent being gone several days fighting fires down in Los Angeles County? Both options had drawbacks, both because of men. Right now, the male sex wasn't rating high on her list.

She finally decided to head to the cabin and pack. Christy approached with trepidation, but there was no sign of Brent's Jeep. Once inside, she grabbed her travel bag and stuffed clothes in it. Cosmetics were shoved into the smaller tote. She made a second trip to collect her astrology books. Ruefully, she thought, *I should have left them at home. Fat lot of good they've done me.*

Lennie's original idea of a horoscope piece for the newspaper was lost in the wake of the murder spree.

Pulling up to the Burlap trailer, she was relieved to see Jacob's car missing. Still, it wasn't clear whether she'd be welcomed as a guest for a second time. Christy decided to leave her baggage in the Saturn and feel out the situation on Lennie's end. Right now, she felt homeless.

Lennie was in the back. Christy located her friend making up the bed in the guest room. "Are the fresh sheets for me?" she asked.

Lennie didn't turn around. "Jacob's been sleeping in here since our little pastry party." She stood up and grinned at Christy. "Not exactly the doghouse, but it's the best I could do."

"Look, Lennie, I didn't mean to cause a rift between you and Jacob. I'm just going to go to the hotel for the rest of my stay. If the county won't foot the bill, I'll pay out of my own pocket."

"Oh, hell no." Lennie crossed her arms and shook her head. "If I have to choose between an uptight jack-wad and my best friend, I know who's winning this one."

They emptied the car and settled down at the kitchen table with a beer and a Dr Pepper.

After clinking the cans together, they toasted the return of camaraderie. Neither mentioned the loss of the men in their lives.

No sense spoiling the moment.

"How's the investigation coming along?" Lennie asked.

"There was a throw-down in the office today between the captain and the lieutenant. It got pretty nasty."

Lennie smiled ruefully. "Those two have a history. Hillard got promoted and Brandt had a tough time swallowing the extra bar."

"That was obvious by Brandt's attitude. Honestly, I thought the captain was going to write him up for insubordination."

"So what was the fight about this time?" Lennie prodded.

Christy hesitated. Brandt's threat lingered in her head. But, since the warning came from Brandt and not somebody she respected, she decided to share.

"First, the lieutenant informed the captain that he had his head up his ass."

"Holy shit," Lennie gasped.

"Oh, it gets worse. Brandt suggested that the locals were all in this together, doing a vigilante justice sort of thing."

"Somebody's been watching too many Charles Bronson movies."

Christy nodded in agreement. "Then one of the deputies came up with a whole conspiracy theory, which really set the captain off."

"Wait a minute," Lennie interrupted. "The deputies witnessed the fight?"

"Um-hm. I forgot to mention we're at task force status now. Sheriff Nolan has Burlap at the top of his priorities."

"And here I thought he was busy running for office again," Lennie sneered.

"Well, he won't get re-elected if he can't stop the murders up here. Not that anyone in the valley really pays attention to the problems in the foothills. Except the TV stations. Even the tabloids are sniffing around headquarters."

A thought entered Christy's head. "Grab your stuff."

Lennie tossed the empty cans in the garbage. "Where are we going?"

"To church."

෴෴

The Rugged Cross rested on top of a small hill with the parking lot at the bottom. This forced the congregation to navigate steep and worn steps to earn their right to worship. Not exactly handicapped friendly.

Going to church was a habit Christy had lapsed out of years ago—a fact her sister Celeste never ceased to nag her about. Christy figured there was enough praying going on at her sister's end to cover the sins of the whole Bristol clan. Sort of like a spiritual blood bank. One contributes and the rest are set for the hereafter.

Compared to the churches of her youth, Rugged

Cross was sparse. Anything compared to a Catholic church would look underwhelming. The whitewashed walls with a stern oak cross, like a giant "T," overlooked the worshipers and brooked no levity. Without stained glass windows or colorful statues of saints, the church felt naked to Christy. It seemed the citizens of Burlap worshiped an uncompromising God.

The benches were adequately uncomfortable but at least, Christy noted, there were no kneelers. Apparently, Protestants were only required to stand and sit during services. Maybe walking up the stairs to be able to worship was punishment enough.

Pews were filling fast. Town hall meetings seemed to have entertainment value in a burg lacking diversions. This one was highly attended by the people of Burlap—except the crippled, aging, and handicapped left at the bottom. Christy spotted Sylvie Hobbs from Hobbs Market, Trudy Meyers, Madge from the Franklin Inn, and a few other locals she'd seen around town. She wondered if the anonymous female caller was mingling with the crowd. Would the snitch dare to come out of hiding?

Chairs were set up behind the lectern. Captain Hillard shifted uncomfortably in his metal seat. Next to him was the public relations deputy, the liaison between citizens and Sheriff Nolan. The mayor of Burlap tried to look stern and concerned but could barely contain his excitement.

Most of the town folk—Burlapians?—eagerly took

the front row seats, as if at a Carrie Underwood concert instead of a community bitch session. Lennie was heading to join them until Christy grabbed her arm and pulled her back.

"Jacob's here," Christy whispered.

She nodded to where the newshound was staked out. His reporter's notepad was open, pen ready, and Linda stood by his side like an eager groupie. Lennie scowled and shrugged off the awkward situation like an old coat ready for a rummage sale.

Reverend Adair came out from the left wing. He mounted the pulpit. "Let us pray."

So much for separation of church and state.

Christy reluctantly bowed her head, praying that the meeting would not continue in a religious vein.

As a community leader, Reverend Adair assumed the role of city manager and watchdog of souls. "We know why we're gathered here tonight, so let's get to it," he irritably announced. He acted as if the meeting was an inconvenience on his time, despite the fact that he'd called for it in the first place. He opened with "Burlap is a cesspool of sin."

"That's an attention getter," Lennie whispered.

"The sin of Cain has made its way into this town and smites the wicked. Four dead, all miscreants, all the tools of the devil."

"Is this a town meeting or a revival?" Christy whispered back.

"I think the reverend is just getting revved up."

Christy gave her friend a sideways glance. "I'll stay until he tries to baptize me."

"These were men who lived in sin, who put poison in their bodies and sold their deadly wares to others," Adair continued. "While I do not condone murder, I cannot mourn those who have died at the hands of evil." Fire and brimstone spewed from his lips.

A local, clearly inebriated, added his two cents. "I believe the murderers are not from around these parts but hippies coming up here to grow marijuana and cocaine."

"And meth stuff," his neighbor chimed in.

"You don't grow meth, you brew it."

"Leroy had been brewing moonshine for years. Nothin' illegal about that."

Men in the crowd hooted with pleasure.

"Where are we?" Christy whispered to Lennie. "The Appalachians?"

Reverend Adair held up his hand for silence. His next words caught everyone off guard. "This town is cursed because of the heathen altars in the hills hereabouts. They are abominations," he declared. "The body of a Mexican growing marijuana on government land was found laid out on the one at Snowshoe Bend as a sacrifice to the devil."

A man in the audience stood and announced, "The aliens done dropped 'um here a century ago. That's what my mama told me."

"Manfred, you're an idiot," an old-timer scoffed. "Yer mama was makin' things up. Those are man-made concrete blocks. Weird lookin' but they don't hurt nobody."

Lennie nudged Christy in the ribs. "It was a Norwegian artist. He was commissioned by the city of San Francisco to create the sculptures and weather-tested them up here. I found an article in the newspaper archives."

"Guess that makes him an alien in their eyes," Christy replied.

The mayor finally jumped up from his seat and urged the preacher to the side. "Order," he demanded. "This is an official meeting, being recorded by Miss Tanent over there. We have minutes, old business, new business, and procedures to follow."

"We didn't come to hear all that malarkey," shouted someone from the center of the crowd.

"You can't speak until I recognize you," the mayor commanded.

"It's Timothy Redbone. You recognize me, Mayor. I'm the one who fixes your truck every time it breaks down. Piece of junk, that's what it is, but you're too cheap to buy a new one."

Snickers went through the crowd.

"Order," the red-faced mayor shouted again. He wisely decided to dispense with formalities. "I have representatives from the Central County Sheriff's Department here to talk about the rash of murders occurring in these parts of late. I want you all to listen and there will be no heckling."

He gratefully turned the audience over to Hillard. The captain introduced himself and assured the crowd that the crimes were a priority for the sheriff's department. He defined the word "task force" and described the manpower and all available resources being dispatched for the investigation. People listened respectfully. There was a sense of pride in the audience, impressed that the happenings of their small town garnered so much attention from the flatlanders.

Hillard turned the lectern over to PR. The deputy was schooled to talk to the public and his manner was laced with concern and commiseration. He begged for patience and the community's cooperation. "We need your help," he intoned, holding his arms out to embrace the audience. "We can't solve these crimes alone. Anyone with information is urged to contact the Crimestoppers Hotline. Your call will be anonymous. You can also contact Area One. Someone is manning the station during business hours and you can leave messages on the confidential answering machine." He proceeded to give out the phone numbers.

"Expect a lot of crazy calls," Lennie warned her friend. "You're going to hear from every person with a grudge fingering their neighbors."

The meeting was opened for questions. They came

hard and fast. Most people railed at the length of time it was taking to find the killer or killers. Apparently, a week to investigate four murders was too long. They demanded to know if there was DNA found at the scene, ludicrous questions stemming from too much CSI on TV. The deputy assured them that state-of-the-art forensic techniques were being used. Christy knew for a fact that forensics in Central County lagged far behind resources accessible in larger cities like San Francisco and Los Angeles. Her rural county didn't have money or manpower to be anywhere near "state-of-the-art." However, this was not what the public wanted to hear or the department wanted to confess. The PR deputy's role was to reassure and pacify people.

A man in a suit and tie stood up to speak. "I'm K.C. McGuire, owner of Sierra Real Estate. I would like to thank the fine detectives of the Central County Sheriff's Department for their diligent efforts to find the perpetrators of these crimes. People looking for vacation homes will be reluctant to invest if they believe this is an unsafe area to reside."

"That's fine with us," someone called out. "We don't want flatlanders moving up here anyways."

"Speak for yerself. I got a store to run," Sylvie Hobbs retorted.

"Okay, we all know nothing is going to be solved tonight," the mayor interjected, trying to wrangle back some control. "I want to thank the sheriff's department and commend them for their efforts to save our community from further violence."

There was weak applause as the captain and the deputy took off as quickly as politely possible.

"Any new business before we close?" the mayor asked wearily as he checked his watch.

McGuire, who had remained standing, said, "Mr. Mayor, I'd like to discuss the dead tree in the middle of Burlap Elementary schoolyard."

"You mean the Buzzard Tree?" The mayor looked surprised that this should even be an issue.

"Yes, the Buzzard Tree. It's an eyesore and a danger to the children."

"Buzzards don't hurt nobody," countered an audience member. "Unless they're dead."

"They eat whatever the kids leave behind from their lunch bags," added another.

But McGuire was not deterred. "The tree is brittle and all you need is a branch to fall on a child's head and you've got a lawsuit on your hands."

The argument had no discernible impact on the audience. Most had eaten peanut butter sandwiches in their formative years under the baleful eyes of the scavengers overhead.

"Plus, it's an eyesore," he added.

"You sure are intent on prettying up this town," Sylvie Hobbs said suspiciously.

McGuire turned and looked at the store owner. "It's

good for your business and brings an infusion of cash into this town's economy. Don't you want Burlap to grow and prosper?

The crowd murmured among themselves as though weighing the pros and cons.

"Not really," one finally volunteered. Heads nodded in agreement. "We like the way things was."

McGuire swiveled to encompass the crowd with his steady gaze. "Change is coming, whether you approve or not," he said with finality.

The meeting closed with nothing accomplished. Christy saw Jacob put away his notepad and take Linda's arm to head down the aisle. He passed Lennie without even a glance.

"Guess I know where he's sleeping tonight," she muttered.

CHAPTER 32

When they got back to the trailer, Lennie went into the bedroom and came out with an armful of Jacob's clothes. She indicated for Christy to open the door and tossed jeans, T-shirts, and ratty sneakers over the handrail of the steps. They littered the front yard like, well, litter. Garbage. The remnants of the latest failed relationship.

"That felt good," Lennie said, looking at her handiwork. "I need a beer."

Over Coors and hot chamomile tea, the women sprawled at the kitchen table. The relationship was finally on an even keel. Everything felt relaxed, familiar.

Christy sighed. "It hasn't even been a week and I feel like I've been up here a month,"

"This has been a hellava week," agreed Lennie. "More excitement than this town has seen in a century."

If you want to call broken relationships, nearly destroyed friendships, infidelity, and a high body count exciting, Christy mused. "I don't need this kind of excitement in my life." She stared into the pale yellow water in her mug. "I want to go home to my boring life, my boring job, and Shamus."

"Okay, Dorothy, then you are going to have to knock those ruby slippers together instead of stomping your foot and whining." Lennie jumped up from the table and disappeared into the back of the trailer.

She returned with Christy's astrology books in her arms.

Rolling her eyes, Christy said, "How is astrology going to get me home? I'm good, but I'm not that good. There's no magic solution between those covers."

Dumping the books on the table, Lennie announced, "You're wrong. You and I are going to find the killer."

"Lennie—"

Lennie sat down on the kitchen chair and leaned forward intently. "Listen to me. I've been listening to you for years and, even though it's just mumble-jumble most of the time, I've picked up a thing or two. Seems to me we could put our heads together and kinda figure out what this killer is like. Then we can match him up with a sign and maybe figure out his birthdate. We'd narrow down the suspects that way."

Lennie was serious. Suddenly, Christy understood what she was saying. "You're telling me we should try to profile a homicidal maniac with astrology? That's just crazy."

"Is it?" Lennie got up and excitedly paced the floor. "Think about it, Christy. How does the FBI profile criminals? They look at their methods and use psychology to try to get a handle on their personality. We've got the planets. You're always saying how a horoscope is simply a tool to understand life and make choices. Plus, you have ESP going on. Let's use what you've got to close this investigation and get you back home."

The scheme was insane. Pure Lennie. Yet, in the corner of her mind, Christy could feel herself getting excited by the idea of trying her hand at a reverse horoscope.

Maybe the whole thing would be an exercise in futility and a waste of time. At least the charting would be a diversion.

Lennie got up and sorted through Christy's astrology books. She picked up the thick white one and handed the volume to Christy. *The American Ephemeris for the 20th Century, 1900 to 2000 at Noon, Revised Edition.*

"Okay. So, what do you want me to look up?"

"The sonavabitch's birthday."

Exasperated, Christy pointed out the obvious. "We don't know his birthday. That's the whole problem."

"Go through your books and figure it out." Lennie

spoke with complete confidence in Christy's abilities. "Which sign feels like a killer to you?"

"Lennie, that's really far-fetched. Look at this." Christy flipped through the pages and showed her friend streams of numbers. "I can't just randomly start doing horoscopes until we find one that fits. We'll all be dead by then."

Lennie fumed with exasperation. "If I could do astrology, I'd do it myself. You've got a gift. Unwrap it and use it."

Christy closed the book and put it on the table. "It won't work."

"Come on, you want to play detective, let's play detective." Lennie picked up the book and shoved it in Christy's hands. "How old do you think the killer is?"

"How am I supposed to know?" Christy retorted.

"Logically, the guy must be in his late twenties to early forties."

"We're assuming the killer is a man?"

"Sure," Lennie said with all the assurance of a lead detective. "Most serial killers are male. Plus, the killer would have to be pretty strong to place the body up on the sculpture."

"Okay, so that gives us a 20-year age span. We're still no closer to a birth date."

"I don't know all the ins and outs of the horoscope, but didn't you explain to me that one of the planets is generational?"

"Pluto. And yes, it's still a planet. The astronomers can shove it." Christy was still sore about the attempt to downgrade Pluto's status.

"Find out where Pluto was hanging out between 1972 and 1986."

Christy looked up the time frame. "Pluto was in Virgo until the summer of '72. The planet moved to Libra and stayed until the summer of 1984."

"Where did it go after that?" Lennie urged.

"Scorpio. But that would make the killer under 27 years old." Quizzically, Christy looked up from the book.

"Then I'm guessing we're looking for a man born with Pluto under either Virgo or Libra." Lennie looked pleased with herself. "Now, tell me what the traits of each sign are."

"Lennie—" Christy started to protest.

"What've we got to lose? Just do it."

When Lennie got stubborn, Christy knew there was no arguing.

"Okay. Virgos are practical, analytical, intellectual, critical, prim, and hypochondriacs." Christy recited the short list of traits by memory.

"Doesn't sound like our killer. Do Libra."

Christy sighed. "Romantic, aesthetic, judicial, lazy, temperamental, and superficial."

"So the guy's a vigilante. He takes matters into his own hands. Maybe he thinks he's filling in where the justice system failed."

"Not all of the victims were criminals," Christy pointed out.

"Maybe to him they were. Drug dealers, drunks, even people on welfare. Some people think that's a crime."

"So, you're saying he's a Republican?"

Lennie wagged a finger. "Too early to figure out his political views."

"Nobody goes around killing people just because they're irritated with somebody's lifestyle."

Lennie gave her a scornful smile. "People kill for less. You know that from working in the sheriff's department."

"So you think this is a vigilante trying to clean up Burlap?" Christy said with skepticism in her voice.

"Not just a vigilante, but a *superficial* vigilante. I'll bet he's hiding right in plain sight. Probably passes himself off as a pillar of the community." Lennie leaned back on the couch cushions and looked pleased with herself. "The murders might be a sort of pattern we don't understand yet."

Christy was uneasy with where the exercise was going. "Lennie, I feel like we're playing God here."

Lennie looked thoughtful. "That's probably how ancient astrologers felt, like they had the key to the universe." She leaned over and tapped the astrology volumes with a finger. "Powerful stuff in those books."

"You have no idea."

Over and over, the zodiac surprised Christy. Her predictions were 98% on the money. But every time she charted someone, she had an uneasy feeling that she was poking her mind where it didn't belong. Yet, she'd been given this ability, some even called it a gift. Christy no longer questioned "Why me?" or "What am I supposed to do with it?" Whatever force pushed her to cast horoscopes, she was past fighting. She'd given in to it a long time ago.

Doing a horoscope in reverse was something new in Christy's experience. Never in any of her books had authors discussed even the remote possibility of turning the tables. Yet Lennie, despite her astrological ignorance, had come up with the idea. It defied logic. Maybe because Lennie was thinking out of the box and, with no preconceived notions, she was the one who thought it up. Christy suddenly found new respect for her friend.

"What planet comes next," Lennie asked, pulling Christy out of her reverie.

"You never studied the solar system in science class?"

Lennie grinned. "Musta skipped school that day. Anyway, I thought the world revolved around me in high school."

"Neptune. This is where it gets tricky." Christy studied the row of numbers and flipped a few pages in the ephemeris.

"Why is that?" Lennie asked, attempting to look over

her shoulder as if the answer was written down on the page instead of a scramble of numbers.

"Well, if we want to go with the idea that our guy is in his mid-thirties, his Neptune would be under the sign of Sagittarius."

Christy had a special fondness for Sagittarians. That was Rodrigo's sun sign. "Sagittarian traits are having a good nature and being logical. But they can also be blunt, fanatical, and intolerant."

"Killing people sounds like major intolerance," Lennie commented.

"Plus, we may be dealing with a fanatic. That ups the ante."

"Tell me about Neptune," Lennie prodded.

How to explain it to a novice? "Neptune makes people search for the 'ideal.' There is yearning and inspiration involved."

"What's the downside?" Lennie pressed. "You always tell me there's a downside to planets and signs."

"Neptune can bring deception and fraud. It also dissolves things, such as relationships."

"Or lives" said Lennie. "I'm nicknaming him 'Drano Man.' He flushes scum right off the earth. What's the next planet?"

"Uranus."

Lennie snickered. "That's the dirty one that made the boys crack up."

"Sophomore humor." Christy flipped the pages of

the ephemeris. "The only sign that fits is Scorpio."

"That sounds pretty evil."

"There is that side of the sign. Scorpios can be revengeful and cold-blooded. Uranus is the planet of opportunity."

"She shoots; she scores!" Lennie yelled, jumping off the chair.

She put out a palm for a high-five, which Christy didn't give her. "Lennie, three planets gets us nowhere. That's as far as we can go."

"Why?" Lennie stopped playing cheerleader. "We're on a roll."

"Because we're down to the faster moving planets: Saturn, Jupiter, Mars, Venus, and Mercury. They move so quickly through the signs that there are too many possible combinations. We'd just be guessing." Christy closed the book. "Not that we're not making guesses already."

"Educated guesses," Lennie corrected.

"We're right back where we started. Nowhere."

"Not quite. I've got another trick up my sleeve." Lennie bounded off to the back bedroom. She came back carrying an old, brown shoebox and wearing the smile of the Cheshire cat.

CHAPTER 33

"When I bought the newspaper, I found this box. Jacob wanted to toss it but it's full of interesting information."

She plunked the box in front of Christy. When she removed the top, the stale smell of old paper wafted out, along with motes of dust anxious to be airborne.

Christy flipped through the large index cards. "What is all this?"

"The old codger who was editor planned ahead. He wrote up obits for everyone in the town. Even his own." Lennie rolled her eyes. "Of course, people have moved into town since then, but not many. And I'm sure the Mexican marijuana growers aren't in here. But we now have a slew of birthdays to check out." Lennie pulled one out and read, "Joseph Langer, born 1961. Navy. Dishonorable discharge. Married to Jennifer Hope in 1970. Logger with Sven Corporation. Predicted demise: alcoholism."

"That reads like a very nasty obituary," Christy said. "How are these obits going to help us find a live killer?"

"Maybe the editor was just staying ahead of the rush." Lennie picked up a few cards. "Look, here's one for Lester Lehman. He wrote 'Drug dealer. Predicted death: homicide.' Wow. He was right on the mark."

"Looks like he updated the cards as time went along." Christy a card at Lennie. "Different ink. Very efficient." She studied the editor's precise writing. She could picture the old man stooped over the stack of index cards, gleefully playing God as he wrote how each would die.

The women divided the index cards between them. There was a temptation to read the brief histories written in the cramped handwriting of the previous publisher. He was thorough in his descriptions and there was an attempt to find the best qualities of each person in Burlap.

"Listen to this: 'Reverend Adair died this week of (fill in later). The reverend was an old fire-and-brimstone preacher and kept our town on the straight and narrow.' Except for the murderers, drug dealers, and assorted vandals," Christy added.

"Okay, I've got one: 'Sylvie Hobbs, a fine citizen of this town, passed on due to (cause of death). Sylvie, proud owner of Hobbs Emporium, was pleasant to all customers and kept us informed of going-ons about town.' In other words, she was the town gossip. Plus, her food was on the edge of the expiration date," Lennie adlibbed. "Her luncheon meat was probably the cause of half the deaths in this box."

They sifted through the cards, separating the ones that fell between the dates they were looking for. Christy pulled Emmons, the bus driver, and Manny Salvatore, bartender at The Jerry-Rig.

"Here's the preacher's son," Lennie commented. "He was born on March 15, 1980."

"The Ides of March," Christy muttered.

"What's an 'ide'?"

Christy looked up, unaware she'd said the phrase out loud. "It comes from the Roman calendar. Julius Caesar was killed on March 15. A soothsayer told him, 'Beware the Ides of March.' Or so Shakespeare wrote."

"Good to know, brainiac."

Christy put the cards down. "This isn't yielding much."

"It's a start." Lennie seemed to be enjoying the snide notations on each subject. "Just think, one of these people might be the killer."

"Yeah, but that doesn't account for all the people who don't have an obit-to-go. Some of the newcomers probably arrived after the editor died. We can't go up to people and say, "We want to write your obituary to save time in the future."

"We could tell them about the astrology column you're going to write."

Christy glared at Lennie. "You know that idea is never going to happen now, right?"

"Okay, what if I go around collecting birthdays and say I'm doing a column called 'Birthday Wishes' for the newspaper?"

Shaking her head, Christy said, "All the women will lie. And, in this day and age, people aren't going to give out that info because of identity theft. It's like asking for their social security number."

"What if—" Lennie locked eyes with Christy. "—you ask Triana to run names for driver's licenses in the DMV database?"

The idea was so unethical, so against department policy that Christy could only stare back, appalled. Not that she hadn't done it before.

"She probably knows how to do it without getting caught. And she has access."

"No way. Remember that lieutenant who ran background checks on his daughter's boyfriends? He thought he was smart by using his secretary's computer when she forgot to log off and went to lunch. They still busted him. He no longer works for us."

"That's because he was running criminal histories. The Department of Justice monitors that database. The state doesn't have enough money to monitor the DMV. Besides, with deputies and detectives going in and out all day, how are they going to know who's using the computer?"

"I'm not going to do it, Lennie."

"You want to solve the case and get back down the hill, right?"

Lennie was putting temptation in her path. Seemed to Christy that several people in her life were making temptation hard to resist these days. "We're operating on hunches here."

"Educated hunches," Lennie replied.

Frustrated, Christy said, "Even if the astrology is right on target, even if we figure out who the killer is, how do you think I'm going to explain that to the detectives on the case? Nobody will believe me, and I'm tired of being laughed at. They already think I'm this crazy broad who believes she can see the future. Why bother investigating at all?" Before Lennie could protest, Christy put her hand up to stop her. "And what judge is going to issue a search warrant with probable cause based on planetary positions? No, Lennie, we aren't going to convince anyone."

"Then we'll just have to flush the killer out using this Box-o'-Death. Once we know who he is, we'll set a trap and catch him."

Or be his next victim, was Christy's gloomy thought.

They spent the next hour going through the cards and

jotting down names that fell into the astrology guideline they had created. Every time Christy found the name of a female with a birthday after 1980, it crossed her mind that she could be looking at a card with the name of the snitch.

When Christy looked up to say something to Lennie, she caught her friend staring hard at a card. "What have you got?" she asked.

"You're not going to like this." Lennie pushed the card across the table. The label was the name "Brent Whatley, Forest Ranger." His birthday fell within the range they were looking for. "Not that he could possibly be a suspect," she quickly interjected.

But Christy was doing some calculations. "Actually, we can't rule him out."

Lennie looked at her in disbelief.

"He was assumed to be out of the area when some of these murders happened."

"Wasn't he fighting fires?" Lennie asked.

"He *said* he was fighting fires." Christy searched for something nagging her memory. "On the night of the hit-and-run, I heard Brent take off in his Jeep in the middle of the night. The time frame fits."

She relayed some of the conversations she'd had with Brent. He had an intense dislike for the petty criminals and lawbreakers who peppered the town. He called them welfare rats, slackers, and squatters. He reserved his best slurs for the marijuana growers and seemed to take it personally that they planted in *his* forest. His tone had bothered Christy, even though his assessment was right.

"But you'd know, wouldn't you?" Lennie pushed. "If you were living with a killer, you'd know. You're ESP would kick in, wouldn't it?"

Good question. Had she been blindsided by his good looks and poetic nature? It was hard to be objective, but she had to try. "Add him to the list," she said reluctantly.

After a bit more shuffling of the cards, Lennie drew in a sharp breath. "Holy crap," she breathed. "Here's a blast from the past. Trace Malin."

Christy grabbed the card. Information was sketchy, but there was no mention of his drug-dealing. "I wondered where he disappeared to after he helped us find info on the sex club."

"Going straight was never Trace's thing. When his parole officer got him the job at the convenience store, I knew it wouldn't last," Lennie smirked.

Even though she worked for the sheriff, Christy found it hard to dislike the felon. When she was at the mercy of Lloyd Parr and his gang of meth makers, Trace had waltzed into the fortress and pulled a con that saved her life. She owed him.

He was a colorful, if not law-abiding, character. Smart, glib, and possibly the most amiable ex-con she would ever meet, Christy had a special place in her heart for the guy. Plus, his crush on Lennie always amused her. She had to admit, there was something intrinsically sexy about Trace. If he'd cut his hair and clean up his act, he might actually have a shot.

"We can eliminate Trace from our list of suspects," Lennie decided.

Christy gave her a worried look. "But he fits the profile of the victims. He could be next. We need to find him and warn him."

CHAPTER 34

Christy drove to the substation in the morning. Only Deputy Espinoza was waiting in the parking lot. He walked over to the Saturn and made a roll-down-the-window motion.

"I'm relieving you today. After last night's town meeting, we're expecting phone calls with tips. The sheriff wants a sworn officer to handle the reports." He didn't sound happy with his assignment.

So now they didn't trust her with information gathering. "Fine by me," she retorted. "What about tomorrow? Do I get a weekend off?"

"Make an appearance in the morning and I'll let you know."

As she drove back to Lennie's place, she worried the

mystery woman might drop a dime to give another elusive message and reach the deputy instead. Even asking to talk to Christy would open a can of worms. Guilt and fear made her nauseous. She'd have a lot to answer for if they found out she'd held back even the flimsiest information about the case.

Lennie was dressed and shoving money into her jeans pocket when Christy entered the trailer. "Didn't expect you back. Who's manning the phones?"

"I've been given a day off."

"How generous," Lennie said sarcastically.

"Are you taking off?" Christy asked, wondering what to do with her free day if Lennie was busy.

"There's a festival at the schoolyard today. I was gonna surprise you at the end of your great vacation up here before all this mess happened."

Christy went to the refrigerator and grabbed a Dr Pepper, even though it was 8 a.m. "I'm game," she said.

"Think so? Wait until you see what's in store. Remember, this is Burlap."

They climbed into the Land Rover and took off down the hill.

Cars were already packing the parking lot and spilling out onto the road. A banner hung from the eaves of the school reading "Turkey Testicle Festival."

"You've got to be kidding me," Christy said.

"Nope." Lennie laughed. "These folks take their balls seriously."

"I didn't even know turkeys had testicles."

Lennie smirked. "City girl, I'll bet you don't even know where a tom keeps his balls."

"Between his scrawny legs?"

"Nope. They keep them under their left wing."

If it ever showed up as a Jeopardy question, Christy would be ready. The day was getting progressively weirder.

"Come on, you're going to have a 'ball.'"

The women got out and started toward a crowd hovering around a booth. The smell wafting through the air made Christy's stomach grumble.

"First stop, pancakes," Lennie announced.

Everyone in town seemed to be jonesing for pancakes. Picnic tables were packed with more people than the town's population. The celebration drew folks from the hills and the woods. Unshaven locals, dressed in faded tee-shirts and well-worn jeans, sat next to retirees in their plaid pants worn with black socks and Birkenstocks. Children ran loose everywhere.

The flapjacks were fluffy and full of fresh blueberries. Cathy Fradenski from the health clinic was at the helm, expertly flipping stacks of pancakes onto the plates of eager breakfasters.

The schoolyard had been turned into a carnival midway. A ferris wheel circled above the crowd, while a rickety rollercoaster traveled its tracks, accompanied by screams of delight and/or terror. There were pony rides and carousel horses for children, a Tilt-a-Whirl for teens. A ring-toss booth, funhouse, and barkers, cajoling people to toss a ball into cups to win a stuffed giraffe, all vied for attention.

A teacher, apparently unpopular, shivered in the dunk tank while the next sadistic student took aim. A kissing booth, manned by two slutty teenagers, had men lined up. Christy wondered if mononucleosis was the prize.

Lennie reeled off the day's activities. "There's a horseshoe tournament this afternoon and a turkey shoot."

Christy stopped in her tracks. "Not live turkeys!"

"Where do you think we get the meat for the chili cook-off?" she answered with a straight face. "While some carnivals have pie eating contests and some have hotdog eating competitions, around these parts there's a different sort of contest, this being the Turkey Testicle Festival."

"You're kidding, right? They don't really eat…" Christy couldn't even get the word out.

"'Fraid so. These hill folk have no shame. Or taste buds. That's why they start drinking early." Lennie nodded toward the Budweiser booth located in the shadow of the buzzard tree. "The men get beer-brave and then it becomes a matter of honor to see who can choke down the most deep fried balls."

Christy felt the pancakes surging for a reappearance. "I think I'm going to lose my breakfast."

"Think of something else. Kittens. Daisies. Think about the Professor 'cause he's headed this way."

"Mornin' ladies," he said with a flourish, spilling suds over the rim of the plastic cup. "How are you this fine spring morning?"

"Christy just found out what we're here to celebrate. She's not feeling too good about it. Me? I'm fine," replied Lennie.

The Professor toasted her and took a swig. "Ah, breakfast of champions."

Three heavily tattooed men walked by, a beer in each hand. They grinned at the trio. The number of teeth between them wouldn't make a full set.

"Do you know what this town needs? A good dentist," Lennie remarked.

"It's been my observation," pontificated the Professor, "that men around here have a tooth-to-tat ratio. Fewer teeth means more ink."

"I think you might have something there," Lennie said, giving him props.

The Professor was on a roll. "Also, I believe sociopathic tendencies are directly related to the distal length of the tattoos." He pointed toward a man, already drunk or high, stumbling across the playground. "See how his tattoos cover his arms all the way down to the wrist? Certified sociopath."

Christy was amused by these assessments. "Sounds like you've put a lot of thought into this."

"What else is there to do in a small town other than study the population? And drugs, of course. Drugs do help."

Detective Razulo would love to hear that tidbit, she thought.

While they enjoyed the raucous and the ruckus of the quickly inebriated crowd, members of Burlap society joined them. Lennie's position as owner of the local paper seemed to give her status. Christy recognized many people from last night's meeting: Preacher Adair and his son, Luke; K.C. McGuire, the real estate agent; Manny, owner of The Jerry-Rig; Postmistress Mona; Emmy, who drove the school bus. Sylvie from Hobbs Market and Madge from the Franklin Inn were familiar faces.

"Enjoying our local customs and cuisine?" K.C. asked in a smooth, car salesman's voice.

"I would enjoy it more if there weren't so many murders," Christy replied.

"She's with the sheriff's department and working with the homicide detectives," Lennie filled in.

Suddenly, the Professor found he had to check out the quilt booth and disappeared into the crowd.

"So, Christy, where are you staying now since they took you out of my motel?" Madge slyly asked.

They had a group smirk at her expense. Apparently, they were aware of the arrangement in the cabin, but not the update.

"She's staying with me," Lennie informed them.

"That trailer of yours is getting a little bit crowded, isn't it?" Mona asked.

Apparently, the whole town suspected there was trouble between Lennie and Jacob and the postmistress was trying to confirm the speculation.

Before Lennie could come up with a tart response, K.C. jumped in. "I'm having an open house next weekend afternoon," he announced. "I'd like to show all of you the projected plans for a new retirement development and proposed golf course. I've got investors lined up. It's going to add quite a bit to the local economy once it's finished."

There were murmurs, both positive and negative, about plans to alter the town's image. But, the lure of free eats was a big draw. After giving out the time, K.C. floated away to invite more of the townspeople.

No longer the center of unwanted attention, Lennie grabbed Christy's arm. "Come on, Christy. You need to check out Karyne Potter's pottery. Maybe you'll find a souvenir to take home from your stay."

"Overpriced, if you ask me," Sylvie groused.

"The goods at Hobbs Market are overpriced, if you want to know the truth," Mona jabbed.

As the argument picked up volume and rancor, Christy and Lennie made their escape.

Colorful booths at the perimeter of the playground displayed various crafts of the townsfolk. The local quilters sold their work—art pieces, really, from large bedspreads to baby blankets. Jars of elderberry jam and wild lupine honey were hawked by rustic women with a sharp eye for tourists. Turkey burgers sizzled on an outdoor grill and people carried turkey legs as if they were lollipops, licking dripping barbecue sauce off their fingers. The chili cook-off area was cordoned off for the competition to come.

"Not exactly a vegan-friendly festival," Christy observed.

"I don't think the locals know non-meat-eaters exist." Lennie nudged Christy. "Looky over there, Miss Trudy Meyers selling her wares. Come on. I've got a bone to pick with her, and it ain't no wishbone."

Cakes, cookies, and cupcakes, homemade fudge and fondant, hand-pulled taffy, and pistachio brittle were on display. A cluster of children surrounded the booth. If there'd been a pane of glass, their noses would have been pressed up against it. Trudy, in her signature pink apron, was doing a brisk business.

"What can I tempt you with, ladies?" Trudy gaily asked as they walked up.

"I hear the banana bread is pretty special," Lennie replied.

A stricken look crossed Trudy's face. Guiltily, she scanned the grounds for a SWAT team to emerge from the crowd. "I—I can explain," she stuttered.

"Oh, and we can't wait to hear it." Lennie said, hands on hips.

"Not here, Lennie. Not now." Christy nodded toward the kids within earshot.

Trudy turned to her helper and motioned for the younger woman to take over. She then guided the women around the booth to her delivery van.

"Look, I made a mistake, okay. I'm sorry," Trudy began.

"You made a mistake, all right. Christy works for the sheriff and you got her stoned out of her gourd. I'd say that was a major error in your judgment."

"I tried to tell you the banana bread was for special customers. You just wouldn't back off. What was I supposed to do?" Trudy pleaded with them, shrugging her shoulders with palms out in supplication. She leaned against the van and sighed. "Okay, I know selling weed is against the law, I know it could ruin my business. It's just that I have one customer with arthritis, another fighting depression, and one on chemo who has trouble holding food down. These people aren't getting high for kicks. I'm not selling to a bunch of teenagers, I'm helping senior citizens in pain. I don't even charge them."

Lennie glanced over at Christy. Awkward.

"How can you afford to do that?" Christy asked. "I mean, drug dealers must be charging you for weed. You don't have a medical marijuana license, and you're not running an official clinic."

"There's a guy, he grows quality cannabis. He's not doing it on government property, he's not farming large quantities, and he gives it to me free in exchange for cookies and cupcakes. I figure he has a serious case of the munchies." Trudy glared at the women. "I'm not giving up the name, so don't ask."

But Christy already knew. "Your friend is Trace Malin."

The surprise on Trudy's face confirmed Christy's suspicions.

"Trudy, listen to me," Christy grabbed the woman's shoulder. "Trace is a friend of ours. We think he's in danger. Whoever this madman is, killing people around here, we don't think he's picking victims randomly. He's targeting people like Trace. We need to warn him to leave, disappear. The investigation isn't getting anywhere, and we're afraid the body count will get higher."

"This isn't some sort of sting, right?"

"No. You've got to believe us. We just want our friend safe."

Lennie nodded in agreement to Christy's words.

Trudy was won over. "Okay, well, he just made a delivery and I don't expect him for another two weeks. I can warn him then."

"That may be too late. You have to contact him now," Christy urged.

Trudy shook her head. "I promised never to go to the grow. He wants to protect me in case the narcs are watching his place." She looked at Christy. "Are they?"

Christy didn't have an answer for her, but she hoped

Razulo and his team didn't have Trace in their sights. If they were, the next move would be disastrous. "Tell us where he's at and we'll go warn him," she said.

Lennie was immediately on board. "Yeah, give us directions. You'll be out of the picture completely. Besides," she added. "Trace will believe us. We have history."

"Doesn't that put you two on the line?"

Christy and Lennie gave each other a look that said *been there, done worse.*

CHAPTER 35

The Land Rover took the dirt road, with all its potholes and brush, like an army tank. Christy tried to hold the directions Trudy had written down steady in her hands, but the bouncing was making her carsick.

"Here, gimme that," Lennie said, snatching the paper and stopping the car. "Stick your head out the window and get a few gulps of air before you lose your breakfast."

As with any good marijuana farmer, Trace had built his operation in a hard to reach location intended to discourage visitors and drug surveillance teams. While the bright green leaves of pot plants were easy to spot from the air by sheriff's helicopter team, dense forest made detection more difficult. This wasn't Trace's first time at the rodeo and, with every failed operation, he gained more knowledge on how to evade the law.

"Okay, I think we're getting close." Lennie handed the paper back to Christy and gassed the vehicle forward. "Look for a rusted wheelbarrow on the side of the road."

"There." Christy pointed.

Lennie parked the Rover and the women got out. There didn't appear to be a path and the forest floor was covered with pine needles that seemed undisturbed for some time. Tentatively, the women moved forward.

"We should have a compass," Christy whispered.

"Why? Neither one of us can read one. It's not like we're girl scouts. And why are you whispering?" whispered Lennie.

"What if Trace has booby traps rigged up?"

Lennie stopped. "That's not his style. Plus, I doubt if they'd be voice activated."

Moving along, they stopped periodically to listen for any non-forest sounds. They were ready to go back to the Land Rover and re-read the directions when they heard whistling. If it was supposed to be mimicking a bird call, the sound fell short of any known bird in existence.

"I think that's supposed to be a warning signal," Lennie said. "We've probably been spotted."

"Which also means Trace isn't alone out here."

"Nope, I'm not alone," confirmed a familiar voice.

Wearing cammies in forest green, Trace emerged

from the shadows holding a shotgun. With the exception of longer hair and a grizzly beard, he looked the same as he did when the women last saw him. At that time, he was working at a stop 'n rob, a convenience store job the narcs got for him after he helped on a drug case. It made his parole officer happy, but nobody ever expected such a dedicated drug dealer to go straight for very long.

Trace lowered the shotgun and grinned at the women. "I've been wondering when you two would come by for a visit. You've been here a week, Christy, and never even invited me up to your cabin."

Lennie grinned. "Well, you haven't exactly been running in her social circles, now have you Trace."

"Oh, I tend to avoid any social circles where members wear badges. I woulda come by to see you, Lennie, but I thought that wussie boyfriend of yours might get jealous." He winked at her.

"How is your illegal crop, Trace?" Christy asked, formalities over.

He glanced uneasily at Christy. "You know about that, huh?"

"We not only know you're growing marijuana, we had a sample."

Trace brightened. "It's primo, right? Man, the soil around here is sweet for growing weed. Best crop I've ever grown. Didn't think that was your thing, Christy, seeing as how you work for Johnny Law. But I can comp you some bud, seeing as how you've done me a solid in the past." He looked at Lennie. "You're rich now, got all that coffee. What about we do a swap?"

Frustrated at his assumption, Christy said, ""We don't do drugs, we got stoned on Trudy's banana bread by accident."

"Oh yeah, Trudy mentioned that. Well, you see, that wasn't supposed to happen. I supply her with product so she can bake sweets for a few people up in the hills for their aches and pains. She also has a few flatlanders with cancer and she keeps them supplied. Now, if the politicians would only lighten up on the medical marijuana issue, we wouldn't have to be sneakin' around and—"

"We don't have time for a political discussion, Trace," Christy interrupted. "We came up here to tell you your life is in danger."

"Nothin' new 'bout that. I live on the edge, girl."

Lennie walked up to Trace. He towered over her five-foot-eleven-inch frame. She took him by the shoulders. "This is serious, buddy. You know about the murders around Burlap?"

"Yeah, yeah, I heard. But I stay away from town for the most part. You don't need to fret about me, darlin'. But it does my heart good to know you have a soft spot for me in yours."

"Now is not the time to flirt, you two," Christy said in frustration. The attraction between her friend and the felon always baffled her.

"Christy's right. We gotta get serious, Trace." Lennie sighed, dropping her hands. "There's a vigilante running around killing people he thinks are 'undesirables.' You need to get out of here because you're the type he's hunting down."

"I know you don't find me 'undesirable,' Lennie." When Trace caught their glares, he stopped being coy. "Look, I 'preciate you ladies coming all the way out here to warn me, but I got a new crop I can't abandon right now. It's planting season and I just got the seedlings in the ground that I need to fertilize and water. There's a lot of work to be done."

Christy gave him a glare. "Your farming could end right here if I notify the narcs," Christy threatened.

They both looked at her.

"You wouldn't do that to me, would you?" Trace begged.

"To keep you alive, yes."

Lennie put her hand on Christy's arm as if to stop her. "He'd be a three-striker, Christy. You can't let him go to jail." She looked crushed.

"If turning him in meant saving his life, yeah, I could do it. In a heartbeat." Christy wasn't sure she meant it, but tried to sound convincing.

Trace leaned against a tree and sighed. "I don't have a life if I'm in prison. I need the sunshine, the open spaces, and my freedom. That's survival."

"You need to stop with all your illegal activities," retorted Lennie. "Would it kill you to go straight for a change?"

He tilted his head and gave her puppy-dog eyes. "Just not in my nature, sweetheart. 'Course, a good woman might make me change my mind."

Lennie seemed to roll the notion over in her mind. "Okay, what if you head down the hill and stay in my place in Kearny? You'll have maid service, all the beer you can drink, and cable TV, but I don't want drugs in my home."

"For how long?"

Exasperated, Christy said, "Until we catch the killer."

Trace turned to look at her. "You girls are gonna catch this murderer? When did you turn into Cagney and Lacey?"

"We got it all figured out with Christy's astrology," Lennie said.

Even to Christy, the idea sounded lame-brained. "We're just playing some hunches. It doesn't matter what we're doing, it matters what you're going to do. Take Lennie's offer. Go down to the valley and live like a king for a while. You might find you like the good life."

"I'm beginning to see your point," Trace said, his eyes glittering at the notion of a little luxury.

Lennie fished in her pocket for her keys and disentangled one to hand to Trace. She gave him the address before the women took their leave. "No drugs," she called over her shoulder.

Once back at the Land Rover, Christy said, "I can't believe you gave him carte blanche to the mansion. Your neighbors are going to go nuts."

"I just hope he doesn't hot-wire the Jaguar or start growing weed in the backyard," Lennie replied. "Charity might begin at home, but when the case is closed, I'm kicking him out."

Strong words from a woman with a weakness for bad boys.

CHAPTER 36

Christy checked in at the substation the next morning. It was only Sunday, but the weekend felt over already.

The office door was unlocked and a deputy she hadn't met before was manning her desk. In front of him were a pile of pink message slips and allegation forms. He looked relieved to see her.

"The phones calls have been steady since the town hall meeting Friday night. Seems like everyone in this town has a beef with their neighbors." He motioned toward the stack of allegations. "I can't believe how many potential serial killers exist in one small town. Oh, and then there's the conspiracy theories. Apparently, the sheriff's department either has a renegade deputy on the loose and we're doing a cover-up or the whole department is under orders to kill off lawbreakers because the jail is too full."

"Well, I'm here now and I'll relieve you." Christy put her purse down beside the desk and waited for him to vacate her chair.

"Wish you could, but my orders are to do background checks for priors on all the names. Guess the captain thinks it's too confidential to hand off to an office assistant. Either that, or they don't want to give you any overtime." He shrugged. "I don't know how you girls do it. If I had to sit all day and answer phones, I'd shoot myself."

Christy gave him the benefit of a doubt that he wasn't being intentionally condescending. She knew his comments merely reflected the general disregard young deputies had for office assistants. With a few more years in the department, he'd soon figure out that to get anything done, he'd better stay on the good side of the women who handled his phone messages, mail, reports, supply orders, and knew all the intel about department politics. Paperwork could easily get "lost," emails "disappear," reports "misfiled," and supply orders "unfilled." A thousand things could go wrong in an office with nobody but "the system" to blame.

Old hands knew the score and made sure to tread lightly, mind their manners, and remember the work wives on Secretary's Day. This youngster, if he wanted to climb the ladder, would catch on—eventually.

She picked up her purse and was nearly out the door when the deputy called out, "I almost forgot. You have a message. Some woman called asking for you. She seemed pissed that you weren't around." He waved the pink message note at her.

Christy went back and took it from his fingers. It had the time and date on it: yesterday morning. The name "Shelley" was scrawled across the top. "Will call back," was the message.

❧❧❧

For now, Sunday was hers. She drove back to the trailer, enjoying the spring flowers covering the hills. When she first got to Burlap, the only flower she could name was lupine, but Brent had educated her on the names the locals gave the blooms. Now she recognized yellow mustard, fiddle-necks, baby blue eyes, the fragile shooting stars, and the yellow star of Bethlehem. Snowdrops covered the hills like a petticoat and once in a while she spotted the white wild violets.

Down in the valley, the Blossom Trail, leading to the foothills, would be attracting tourists, eager to see the peach, nectarine, and plum trees bursting with color. Along with the beauty came hay fever, for which the valley was notorious. The pollen index rose to outrageous heights, encouraged by the warming weather and accompanying breezes. She didn't miss the sneezing and watery eyes, or the haze that hugged the valley floor from car exhaust and dust from farmers planting fields. The visit to Burlap could have been a pleasant experience if it hadn't lasted so long, created tension with Lennie, screwed up her relationship with Rod, and, oh yeah, all those dead bodies showing up.

Lennie was just getting out of bed when Christy got back to the trailer. "Another day off?" her friend asked while stumbling toward the coffee pot.

"I think the sheriff is trying to save overtime," Christy groused. "One of the deputies is covering the phones and handling the allegation calls. It's not rocket science."

"I don't know why they don't turn you loose and let you go home. Shamus must miss you."

Christy thought about her teenage kitten. "I think he's in good hands with Trina. She's not going to spoil him like some people I know."

"Hey, that's what aunties are for," Lennie said, not at all apologetic for all the toys she showered on the feline or the catnip to feed his addiction. "What's on the agenda for today?"

Christy headed for the fridge and took out her breakfast Dr Pepper. "I don't know," she muttered. She pulled out the pink message slip and waved it in the air. She'd already told Lennie about the mysterious woman. "The snitch is trying to contact me. I don't know what she's going to do since I've been MIA for the last two days."

"When are you going to tell the captain about your source?"

Christy dropped into the kitchen chair. "I don't know how to do it at this point. I'll get reamed for not handing her over to the task force at the beginning of the investigation even though she would have disappeared on us. I'm not sure if her info is even reliable. She's convinced there is a conspiracy and even believes a deputy is involved."

"That's a reach." Lennie poured herself a cup of coffee and doctored it to the point of mostly cream and sugar. "The guys can pull some shenanigans, but none of them are corrupt."

"Except for the former sheriff who sold county vehicles to a private security firm."

"That was more stupid than corrupt." Lennie sipped her coffee. "What about Razulo? Shouldn't it have been his responsibility to come forward with the fact that there was a confidential informant in the mix?"

"That opens up another whole can of worms." Christy finished her soda and crushed the can with her hands. "Remember, there's still the missing tape." Two careers potentially destroyed by one skittish snitch.

Confident as always, and sure of a solution, Lennie said, "Well then, girlfriend, we're just going to have to track down the killer. The brass will hate you for showing them up. Or, if you want, I can take the credit. I mean, what can they do—fire me?"

It was a terrific solution except all they'd hit were dead ends and astrological speculations. No, the key was Shelley. Christy knew they had to literally draw her out of the woods and get her to come forward to the authorities with vital information.

But how much did the snitch really know? She'd pointed the finger at Razulo, convinced that the detective was behind the killings. She'd heard Razulo make a verbal threat and taken it as proof.

But Shelley also pointed a finger at Brent. He hadn't been exactly sympathetic toward squatters, pot growers, and drunks cluttering up his woods. It was a side of him Christy was startled to be exposed to when she heard him refer to them as "trash" and "welfare dregs." Would he go so far as permanently erasing undesirables from the area? She hoped she was a better judge of character. Wait—she was the one seduced by literary prose before cheating on a man who loved her. Her own character was questionable.

Christy remembered the night Brent slipped away from the cabin the same night of the hit-and-run. At the time, it didn't occur to her to connect the two incidents. But now?

Maybe it was a coincidence or maybe it was something more sinister. "Now I'm the one seeing conspiracies," she muttered.

"What's that?"

Christy realized Lennie was waiting for an answer.

"No, you can't take the fall for this. I have to come clean."

Wryly, Lennie said, "Confession might be good for the soul and this is Sunday. But the head honchos won't be around until after briefing tomorrow. Meantime, why don't we go to Ronnie's Roadhouse and grab some breakfast. Consider it the last meal of a condemned woman."

❧❧

Ronnie's, known for its fluffy biscuits smothered in a glutenous white gravy thick as mashed potatoes and peppered to the point of no return, was prepping for the after-church crowd. The Professor sat at his usual table, sipping herbal tea and nibbling on an English muffin. A few bleary-eyed campers shuffled in, hankering for pancakes and padded booths after days of cooking over a grill in Kings Canyon National Park. They smelled like wilderness: fir trees, wood smoke, unwashed bodies.

Lennie led Christy to a table with a window looking out to the parking lot. A young woman, barely past her teenage years, sauntered up to their table with a coffee pot in hand. She didn't ask, just cocked an eyebrow and both women nodded. After pouring, the waitress pulled two menus from under her arm and slapped them on the table. She walked off without saying a word.

"Courtesy is extra," said Christy.

"So is a tip." Lennie looked over the laminated folder, sticky with fingerprints from previous diners. "Go with the waffles and seasonal fruit. I can't vouch for anything else."

Christy nodded. Better safe than salmonella.

As they waited for their food and nursed their third cup of coffee, people from town drifted in. Most were dressed in their Sunday best, outdated fashion but clean and pressed. Many of the men wore clip-on ties and swapped out tennis shoes for scuffed dress shoes. Children rushed in, eager to smear their clothes with blueberry syrup and knock over glasses of orange juice. The decibel level went up several notches as toddlers let loose with screams they'd had to contain during church services. The waitress walked through the bedlam, carefully avoiding kids underfoot and maintaining a bored exterior.

"How are you ladies doing?" Standing over their table was K.C. McGuire. He had a suit on, dressed for success even on a Sunday. His smile was the same one that beamed out from billboards advertising foothill properties. Warm. Reassuring. Not exactly genuine, but passable.

Without asking, he slipped into the booth beside Lennie. She reluctantly scooted over and gave Christy a look that said, "Can you believe this guy?"

"Christy, right? I thought you'd be heading home by now," he said.

"Yeah, me, too."

The waitress brought their plates of waffles to the table. She looked at McGuire. "You need a cup?"

"That's the way I like to drink my coffee," he replied. He laughed heartily at his lame joke and watched them pass the syrup back and forth then dig into their waffles. "So, how's the investigation going? Any suspects?"

Christy took her time chewing, swallowing, and washing the mouthful down with coffee. "I can't really talk about it."

"Everybody's talking about it. In fact, that's the topic du jour." He laughed again, a hollow guffaw. "Not that murder's a laughing matter," he quickly corrected himself. "It's just the most exciting thing to happen in this neck of the woods."

"We take homicide very seriously," replied Christy.

He turned his attention on Lennie. "Well, your little newspaper must be having a field day. The *Bag* has an exclusive. You're right in the middle of the action."

"The sheriff's department has blocked us out. We get the same reports as the rest of the media." Lennie shrugged and forked a piece of pineapple in her mouth. Canned fruit was in season year around.

"Well, the reason I stopped by your table is to invite you to a little party I'm having tomorrow night at The Jerry-Rig. I'm turning the big 4-0, officially over-the-hill. I'd love to see you two beauties there to celebrate with me. Party starts at 7 o'clock. Early, I know, but it's a work night. The town rolls up the sidewalk by 10 p.m."

Lennie eyed Christy before replying, "We'll check our social calendars. I think we might be free."

McGuire gave them a wink and wandered off to table hop.

"Well, isn't that interesting," Lennie drawled.

"What—that he's throwing a party for himself?"

Lennie turned to look at her friend. "No. It's interesting that he's an Aries and he's forty years old. He fits our profile."

CHAPTER 37

They raced back to the trailer. Christy couldn't wait to pull out the ephemeris and cast K.C.'s chart. He was one of the few in town who didn't have a ready-made obituary because he was a newcomer. Flying under their radar, the women hadn't even considered him a possible suspect.

"There's still no motive," Christy reminded her friend.

"Just chart the sucker. Maybe the motive will show up." Lennie pulled up to the trailer, a swirl of dust in her wake.

As they were getting out of the car, Christy heard a hiss from behind one of the bushes along the driveway. She walked over and nearly stumbled over a young woman in a crouch. The woman looked up at her, face dirty, clothes torn, and the rank odor of fear-sweat emanating from her body.

"What's going on," Lennie demanded, peering over Christy's head.

"Are you Shelley?" Christy asked quietly.

The young woman nodded. A tear streaked down her face.

"Better get you inside." Christy looked around, making sure there were no prying eyes.

Once inside the trailer, Lennie sat the woman down at the kitchen table and brewed a pot of coffee. She popped bagels in the toaster and poured a glass of orange juice. "You look cold and hungry. Let's get you taken care of."

So far, Shelley hadn't uttered a word. She kept her eyes on Christy, trusting but wary. Christy returned the gaze, trying to trust, definitely wary. It was one thing to converse on the phone, but a line had now been crossed. Meeting with an informant without authorization was breaking more than a few rules.

Lennie placed the plate of bagels in front of Shelley. The woman looked at them blankly, not sure what to do.

"Never eaten a bagel?" Lennie asked. She grabbed one and slathered cream cheese on it. "It's Jewish food. You're gonna love it. Try a bite."

Shelley snatched it from her hand and hungrily bit in. The look on her face was one of sheer pleasure. Christy had a feeling that a piece of stale bread would have produced the same effect. The woman had apparently gone without a decent meal in a while.

The hot coffee stopped Shelley's hands from shaking. After she seemed calm enough, Christy started the questioning. "What's going on, Shelley?"

"My real name is Patricia."

"Okay, good to know. How did you know where to find me?"

Patricia shifted uncomfortably. "I've been watching you. I know you aren't in the cabin anymore so I figured you came here to your friend."

"I'm Lennie." She put her hand out and Patricia wiped her palm on her jeans before shaking.

"I'm glad you finally came forward," Christy pressed.

"I think my life is in danger."

Alarm bells went off in Christy's head. She felt her skin prickle.

"Why? What did you do?"

"I didn't do anything," Patricia protested. "I overheard a conversation I wasn't supposed to hear."

"You were eavesdropping?"

"No, I was going to take some food out of the garbage at The Jerry-Rig. The waitress there wraps up leftovers from happy hour and leaves them out for me. That's when I heard two men talking in the office. The window is right over the dumpster."

Christy shoved aside for the moment the idea of anyone living on kitchen scraps. "What were they talking about and why do you think you're in danger?"

"I heard them say they just had to get rid of the rest of the riff-raff before their plans could go through."

"What kind of plans?"

"I don't know," Patricia said, exasperated. "I don't care. But they said they needed to get rid of me because I was Lehman's bitch. That's what they called me. His bitch."

The woman was clearly offended, although Christy was sure she'd been called worse. "Could you tell who was talking?"

"Manny, the bar owner. The other man was that guy who sells vacation homes to rich people."

K.C. McGuire. What a coincidence. No, not a coincidence at all. The horoscope profile was on target, despite her skepticism. Christy realized Patricia was at the end of her rope and couldn't keep one step ahead of the killers while the detectives followed weak leads and chased their tails. Eventually, Manny and K.C. were going to find her. Other than an overheard conversation and a fictitious astrology chart, there was no proof to back up the claim that a business owner and a prominent member of Burlap society were orchestrating the rash of murders.

"It's time you came forward and started talking to the detectives," Christy said

Silence.

"Look, you either trust us or you don't."

"And then what?" challenged Patricia.

"I don't know. There's going to be a lot of questions and some pissed off officers but you'll be safe. That much I can guarantee."

"What if they don't believe me?"

Lennie nodded. "She's not the most credible witness. There's no proof. No motive. Unless the captain believes in astrology, which I'm sure he doesn't, you two haven't got shit to show him."

"They said they wanted the land," was Patricia's sullen reply.

That's what this was all about? A land grab? Hell, most of the victims didn't own any land—at least not legally. They squatted, just like their fathers did before them. They seemed, to Christy, clannish and rebellious to the demands of society. Cantankerous. Ignorant. Stubborn. Tenacious. Not the best breed of neighbors, but surely not worth killing.

They decided that Patricia badly needed a bath and clean clothes before Christy transported her to headquarters. Finally, Christy was going back down the hill, back to the valley and home. Once Patricia was the watch commander's problem, she'd be out of the grasp of the homicide team. Freedom!

It was a new woman who appeared from the bedroom. Patricia cleaned up well. With fresh clothes and clean hair, she didn't look like a dumpster diver or drug addict. There was still a scared rabbit look in her eyes, but her face no longer appeared haggard. Amazing what a little soap and water could accomplish.

"Do you want me to do anything?" Lennie asked as Christy climbed into the Saturn.

"Call the watch commander and tell him I'm bringing in a witness. It's his call whether he wants to notify Hillard on a Sunday. And call my roommate and tell her I'm coming home."

CHAPTER 38

Patricia fidgeted in the passenger seat, getting more agitated as Christy negotiated the winding roads.

"Is my driving that bad?" Christy tried to sound lighthearted although she was nervous navigating the foothills.

"I don't know if I want to do this."

"Too late for that. I can't keep covering for you."

Patricia turned to her. "But what if they don't believe me?"

It was a valid concern. There was a standing "us against them" mentality in law enforcement, twice as bad with narcotic and homicide detectives. They were trained to be suspicious. It was what kept them alive. Every day they sorted through lies and deceptions to get to the truth.

Everyone was a suspect until proven innocent. Sometimes even that was not enough.

Christy jerked the steering wheel and attempted to make a U-turn in the middle of the road. The roadway was too narrow and she had to go into reverse to swing around. Thank God there was no traffic.

"What the hell are you doing?" Patricia yelled as she grabbed the dashboard. "Are you crazy?"

"We're going to K.C.'s office."

"Oh, you don't believe me. You want to ask him yourself if he wants me dead?"

Christy glanced over, exasperated. "We need proof to substantiate your story. We need something to get the detectives to take your accusations seriously."

"But what if he's there? If he's willing to kill me, what makes you think you're safe?"

Good question. "I saw him earlier at the restaurant. He could be there awhile."

Patricia wasn't thrilled with the detour and she simmered in silence. Christy concentrated on the road ahead. She was about to commit a B and E, breaking and entering. What was a felony offense on top of all the other rules she'd broken at this point?

'*It's the right thing to do.*'

Celeste. '*Now you want to weigh in?*' Christy communicated irritably.

'*Didn't think you wanted my input.*'

ESP certainly beat out cellphones. '*So you're okay*

with what I'm about to do? Doesn't sound like a nun.'

'*It's for the greater good.'*

Christy sighed. Of course, Celeste would take the long view. It wasn't as if she could ever get fired from her job. Excommunicated maybe. Did nuns get unemployment?

'*I can hear those thoughts, you know.'*

Damn.

'*Better concentrate on your driving. You're a lousy driver and these roads are treacherous.'*

'*God is my co-pilot.'*

'*Don't blaspheme. Just drive.'*

Which is exactly what Christy did. Braking, turning, gaging her speed, heart in her throat the whole time. Cursing Patricia for putting her at risk. Cursing the whole homicide team for their selfish abuse. Cursing Lennie for ever inviting her to come and visit. Wanting to wash her hands of everything and go back home to her boring job and her cat. Wishing this could be over with.

Pulling up to the A-frame, Christy saw that there was no car in the parking lot. "I don't know how we're going to break in. Maybe I should throw a rock through the window. I mean, how can I get into any more trouble than I'm already in?'

Patricia surprised her by jumping out of the car. "You're really stupid, you know that?" She pulled out an eyeglass case and extracted several small tools. They looked like something from an eyeglass repair kit.

The woman headed for the front door.

Christy ran to catch up. "What are you going to do?"

"I'm picking the damn lock. How do you think I survive out here? I can get into any place I want unless there's a really good deadbolt. Only vacationers bother to install those. Locals don't care."

Patricia squatted down in front of the doorknob and within seconds had the door ajar. "I've picked this one before when a gay couple owned it. I guess you know how welcome they were in Burlap."

Christy didn't know what she was looking for. A hit list would have been convenient. She shuffled through documents on the desk, mostly promo ads for *The Kearny Sun's* Sunday real estate section. Cabins to rent with spring discounts, homes to buy, acreage for sale. The ads were attractive, the prices listed were well below nearby Sierra Nevada properties. "Nature Right In Your Own Backyard," read one slogan; "A Town Growing With Your Needs," announced another. *Not to mention a growing mortality rate,* Christy added ruefully.

Tacked up on a bulletin board were artistic renderings by someone who'd probably never set foot in Burlap. K.C.'s vision of the planned community was ambitious. Hobbs Market was replaced by a Whole Foods. There were fountains and a gazebo in the middle of a sculpted town square. The pottery shop was still there, as well as the candy house. Karyne and Trudy had passed inspection. The post office doubled as a stationary store.

Art shop, Starbuck's, a pricey resort clothing store, a sports outlet for fishermen and hunters, next to a nature museum. The new Burlap offered everything city folk needed to live comfortably.

There was nothing the existing residents and old-timers could use or afford.

It wasn't hard to foresee the problem with all these affluent ideas. Burlapians would dig their heels in and try to hold on to the ground as their pappys had done for decades. They never considered themselves squatters. That was an idea civilization had foisted upon them. The land was theirs, had been all of their life, long before anyone took notice of this poor patch of foothills. Ignored by the rest of the world, the residents in turn ignored details like deeds and property taxes. Rules didn't apply and nobody from the government bothered to enforce them. Considering it too much trouble and expense to tangle with the natives, agencies closed their eyes and hoped problems would simply go away.

Next to the renderings of the futuristic town was a map similar to the one at headquarters. A drawn circle intersected areas owned or squatted on by the murder victims. Penciled in was "golf course." She was familiar with that map and now she knew the significance. K.C. wanted to build a golf course to attract new property owners. The quality of the populace would go up and so would the price of land.

The only things standing in his way were the derelicts and undesirables. He'd found a permanent solution to the problem.

"I'll be damned," she exhaled. Without bothering to pull out the push pins, she ripped the map off the wall and crumpled it in the middle with her hand. "Let's get out of here."

On the desk was an answering machine cassette tape. She grabbed that as well.

Running to the car, they both saw a dust cloud on the road. The SUV came around the curve. K.C. was alone. Christy and Patricia piled into her car and Christy threw the map over the seat out of her way. She hit the gas and sent gravel spewing in her wake.

"He saw us." Patricia glanced back, fighting with the map to get a clear view through the back window.

"Maybe he thinks we just stopped by and left when he wasn't there." A long shot, but it was all Christy could come up with.

"No, he's following us." Patricia swung back around. "How fast does this thing go?"

"Not fast enough."

The Saturn was doing its best, as was Christy. Speed picked up on the downhill curve. Christy could feel the car careening out of control and her nerves were just as unsteady. Instinctively, she tapped the breaks.

All of sudden, a shadow filled the window. The Tahoe pulled alongside. K.C.'s face glared at her with unmistakable fury.

He doesn't even know I've got the map and he's coming after me.

The grim look on his face, clenched jaw, and hate in his eyes signaled cold rage. That's all it took to confirm her suspicions and everything Patricia had told her. His next move was more proof than Christy needed. He pulled the wheel hard and slammed into the Saturn.

"Oh my God, he's trying to run us off the road," Patricia screamed.

The narrow roadway didn't have any guard rails to stop the car from diving down the side of the cliff and into the trees. The car shuddered as the vehicle slammed into metal again.

Christy could feel the front tire wobbling as she tried to keep the car on the road. It was impossible to go any faster.

To her relief, a car was headed up the hill. K.C. would have to make a decision to either pull ahead, fall behind, or meet the oncoming car head-on.

With seconds to spare, the SUV pulled ahead as if passing the Saturn.

In that brief moment respite, Christy realized where she was. She screamed at Patricia, "Hold on, we're going down," and guided the car off the road and onto the prison service road.

The quick turn and narrow dirt path was too much for the damaged front. "Get ready to jump out," Christy panted. "Make for the trees on your side and keep going.

One of us has to reach the guardhouse. Get help."

The Saturn limped as far as it could go, listing as the tire shredded to the rim. The women flung open the doors and scrambled for cover in the forest.

They were too late. Above their heads, shots shattered the silence.

CHAPTER 39

Christy kept running, hoping Patricia was out of rifle range or at least hidden by dense growth. Thank God, the woman was wearing muted colors that acted as camouflage. Christy cursed her white shirt and wished she'd put on her Nikes this morning instead of flats. She kept losing her footing. More than once she found herself on her ass, scraping her hands, as she tried to stop the downhill slide. Tears stung her eyes and made things blur when she needed to have sharp focus.

Another shot rang out.

Stumbling, she found a tree large enough to hide behind and catch her breath. It was hard to tell how far away her pursuer was. The crack of gunshots echoed in the forest, disorienting her sense of direction. Although she felt she'd put some distance between her and K.C., there was no way Christy could know for sure.

At any rate, he could only chase one of them on foot. Patricia was younger, quicker, and had an advantage over both of them. The woman was used to hiding out and was familiar with the terrain, having grown up around here. McGuire had probably already figured this out. Which made Christy the easier prey. Also, who would believe Patricia's accusations if the woman made it to safety? Christy had kept the snitch's secrets a little too well.

Panting, Christy launched herself away from her hiding place and ran/stumbled farther down the side of the hill. She grabbed tree trunks for balance whenever she could, wincing as rough bark bit into her scraped palms.

The silver glimmer of the Kings River teased through the trees. If she could make it to the bridge leading to the prison camp, she might be able to reach the guard house and get help. But she would be exposed, an easy target. Found with a bullet in her back wouldn't cause anyone to conclude she was murdered. Hunting accidents happened all the time in the foothills.

A crack of a branch caused Christy to snap her head in the sound's direction. Patricia was farther down the slope and nearly to a flat part of the terrain. The guard was standing on the bridge, alerted by the gunfire. Patricia lifted her arms in a frantic wave to catch his attention.

The salvation Christy felt was cut short as she saw Patricia jolt forward and drop dead-weight to the ground.

The delayed crack of the deadly shot rang in Christy's ears. With the instincts of a rabbit, she dived for the nearest bush and rolled herself into a ball. She was still in his sights but hoping to be the smallest target possible.

She prayed McGuire would make a run for it before the guard called for help. But no, he'd have to make sure she was dead. She was now the only witness, and even if it was her word against his, the detectives would believe her. Plus, she had the map. And she had Razulo to confirm the contact with Shelley/Patricia.

Patricia. Although they'd only just met in person less than an hour ago, Christy felt an overwhelming responsibility for the woman's death. It was a dangerous game Patricia played with dangerous people. But, for whatever reason, she'd chosen to trust Christy. *And I couldn't help her.* The only retribution would come by staying alive and making the snitch's sacrifice mean something.

There was rustling above her hiding spot. Too close. She had to decide: make a run for it or stay in a ball and hope for the best.

"I know you're out there," McGuire hoarsely called. "You can't hide. I'll find you."

The explosion of gunfire made her jump. It was farther away than she placed him. Maybe she could make a run for the large tree yards ahead.

Before she could move, another shot rang out. This one was much closer, enough to make her ears ring.

The rat-a-tat of exchanged gunfire echoed throughout the forest. Christy cringed and covered her ears. She held her breath and waited for the impact of bullets. *Please make it quick and painless*, she prayed.

When silence came, it was nearly as deafening. She heard the crash of brush and a voice calling her name.

Razulo's grizzled face appeared above her. He reached out and she snatched his hand. His grasp was strong and sure, his face strained.

"McGuire?" she asked.

"Dead," he replied.

Nausea overwhelmed her. She bent over and lost her breakfast while Razulo held her by the shoulders.

"Patricia," she gasped.

"Who?"

"The snitch." She pointed to the spot where she saw the woman fall. "She's been shot."

Razulo immediately left her and headed down the hill. The guard was nearly to the body. He had a hand radio and was calling in, hopefully for an ambulance and not the coroner.

Dizzy, Christy attached herself to a tree trunk and tried to steady herself. She felt caught between the two corpses and was afraid to leave this spot of safety and sanity. Somebody was going to have to eventually pry to her from the redwood.

The pursuit and shoot-out felt like it had lasted for hours, but the noon sun was overhead. Christy's body was shaking, but not from the cool coverage of the forest.

Adrenaline? Shock? She closed her eyes and tried to blank out the horror of what had happened and what might have been.

"Are you okay?" Razulo stood a few feet away, his arms helpless at his side.

She nodded. "Is Patricia going to make it?"

He shook his head. "Touch and go. She took a bullet to the spine. They've called an ambulance." The detective pointed down the slope where several guards were carrying Patricia out on a litter. "Let's get you out of here."

Razulo routed her in a wide semi-circle around K.C.'s body. Christy saw his shoes and shifted her eyes away. *His fortieth birthday tomorrow,* she thought. Some of his victims hadn't made it to forty.

CHAPTER 40

Word had gone out and detectives were already on their way to Burlap. Razulo took Christy to the substation where Espinoza put a mug of strong coffee in her hands. The warmth helped steady her and gave her something to concentrate on. The deputy watched her as if she was bone china ready to shatter any second now.

She soon heard tires screeching on the gravel. The homicide team trooped in by singles and doubles. Although eyes searched her for signs of a break-down, they could barely contain their excitement over catching the killer. The fact that an office assistant was the one to put her life on the line rubbed a few egos and there would be a grilling ahead.

Christy was pretty sure they wouldn't like what she would spill.

For now, the team was respectful. They asked about her injuries, not just physical but probing for a mental collapse. They were trained to deal with gunfire, although they seldom discharged their weapons in the line of duty. When a deputy killed someone, a trained peer rushed to the scene as a shock absorber. There was nothing in place for the mental health of support staff.

Don't cry, Christy admonished herself. That was what the men were expecting and she wasn't going to give it to them. Tears were for later.

There was a scuffle at the doorway. Wolfe pushed detectives aside, Lennie in tow. Lennie rushed forward and clasped Christy in her arms. Wolfe, for all his faults, knew exactly the support Christy needed.

"Lennie, it was awful," Christy whispered. "Patricia's been shot, McGuire is dead, and I think I wrecked the Saturn."

"Shh," Lennie said, pulling bits of dirt and brambles out of her friend's hair. "All of that is for later. Let's get you out of here." She locked eyes with the circle of men, daring them to differ.

Lieutenant Brandt blocked their escape route. "We need to debrief her."

"That's not a priority right now," Captain Hillard countered. "We can do that back at headquarters."

Brandt looked around the room for support but all

eyes shifted away from his glare. It was clear who was in charge this time.

Lennie bundled Christy into the Land Rover and the investigative team filed out to the yard to see her off. Wolfe waved them away with a jaunty salute.

"Some vacation, huh?" Lennie, as usual, was trying to diffuse the situation with wild understatement.

"This has all turned out so wrong." Christy heard the jitter in her voice and knew waterworks were on the way.

"You could say that. On the other hand, you solved the case."

"I got two people killed in the process." Tears streamed down her cheeks. She wiped them away with the back of her hand. A contact lens spilled out and was lost somewhere in the vehicle.

Through the blur, she made out a car parked in front of the newspaper's trailer as they pulled up. A man leaned against it, arms crossed.

"You've got a welcoming committee," Lennie said, grinning.

Rodrigo stepped forward and opened the passenger door. He took Christy's arm and gently guided her out of the car. With a nod to Lennie, he guided Christy up the steps of the trailer and settled her down on the couch. He went to the kitchen, returned with a Dr Pepper, popped the lid, and handed it to her.

"How did you know about the accident and everything else?" she asked between gulps.

"Trina called me after you said you were coming home. Then Wolfe had your dispatch call about the shooting. I got up here as fast as I could."

"I think it's time you got her back home," Lennie said. She noted the tension between her friends and slipped off to the bedroom.

"I'm sorry for everything, Rod," Christy started."

"Let's save 'sorry' for later."

Christy nodded. She was too strung out for a sensible conversation. Right now, the cold sting of the soft drink was the only thing she fixated on. Recovery started with familiar routines.

Lennie came out with the overnight bag and the astrology books. Rodrigo rose to take them from her and left the room. Lennie went into the kitchen and grabbed two more cans of soda.

"For the trip home," she said, thrusting them into Christy's hands. "You're going to need a backup."

Christy nodded. The trip down the hill was sure to be long and tense.

CHAPTER 41

The open window whipped her hair and the coolness stung her eyes. She stared out at the forest, beautiful but now deadly. Would she ever admire a redwood again without remembering how she clung to the bark of one while the woods reverberated with gunfire?

She turned to say something to Rod, break a crack in the ice between them. With one eye clear and a blur from the other, she spotted the tail of a dark blue car peeking over the decline of a steep hill.

"My Saturn," she moaned. "Stop. I need to see the damage."

Rod kept his eyes staring straight ahead. "No. You've seen enough for one day." His lips were in a tight line. There was no arguing with that set face.

Feeling like she'd been scolded, Christy opened another Dr Pepper. As she sipped, she tried to sort out where his anger was coming from. She'd just been through one of the worst ordeals of her life, yet he wasn't giving her comfort. He'd appeared out of nowhere like the proverbial knight in shining armor, but he now wouldn't look at her or say the words she longed to hear. Was he pissed that he hadn't been the one who "saved" her, Razulo instead acting as a stand-in? Not the time to play the macho card.

Or was the scene in the cabin with Brent still front and center in his mind? Trust, something both held as crucial in their relationship, seemed to have vanished. Christy knew it was entirely her fault and she'd have to live with one weak moment for the rest of her days. It could cost her the most important love of her life. The damage was done and worse than he imagined. Or maybe his imagination had conjured up far worse scenarios.

With nothing to do on the trip home but mentally reprimand herself, Christy unwilling examined exactly why she'd been unfaithful. It was easy to romanticize the situation: isolated forest, cozy cabin, the wine, the meal, the man, the words of Thoreau. She'd been seduced by the ranger's rapt attention. Plus, she'd been unhappy, alone, and feeling abandoned. Who wouldn't cave in, under the circumstances? Lennie would have jumped in the sack without a second thought.

She wasn't Lennie. She was a plain girl who had finally convinced herself she was pretty. A pair of contact lenses, a new hairstyle, and finding out she could attract another good-looking guy had gone right to her head. She'd allowed herself a vanity never before experienced. For the first time, she wasn't just the "smart" girl but the one boys looked at.

I am so shallow. She glanced over at Rod's profile. Just like the first time she'd seen him, undercover as a Colombian drug dealer, she was stunned with his looks. Hair, black as night, curling at the slender neck. Eyebrows, dark, thick, shadowing his sable eyes. The straight nose, the dimple on the right side of his cheek. Lips, too soft for his the rest of his strong features. A mustache now, sometimes a goatee, whatever his DEA personae required. And his skin, the color of latte, smooth, musky, better than any man-made cologne.

He was what made her feel beautiful.

They were getting closer to Coronita. Excitement was building as she realized she would be reunited with Shamus, hoping the kitten wouldn't be too spoiled. She'd soon be in her own apartment, her own bed, her life. How long would the department give her before shuttling her off to headquarters? How many rules had she broken? Would she still have a job after they learned the extent of her involvement with the snitch? As the car pulled up to the yellow Victorian house, Rod finally turned to her. "'The mass of men lead lives of quiet desperation.'"

Christy looked at him, stunned. "That's from 'Walden.' I didn't know you read Thoreau."

"There's a lot you don't know about me."

He popped the trunk and got out her bag and books. He handed them to his cousin Trina who'd come racing out of the house to welcome her roommate home.

"Hey, aren't you coming in?" Trina asked him as he opened the car door.

Rodrigo looked at Christy and shook his head. Then he drove away leaving the two women in the dust.

✶✶✶

The grilling at headquarters was a bad as anticipated. The sheriff was in attendance as well as Hillard and Brandt.

In her corner was Sergeant Traynor, loudly defending his office assistant. "You forced her to stay up there, against her will, and she winds up solving the case. Now you want to write her up?" he boomed.

"She was getting info and not passing it to the commanding officer," Brandt hollered back.

The sheriff intervened. "She isn't authorized to communicate with informants. She should know that."

"Patricia wouldn't talk to anyone else. She was afraid the killer might be one of the deputies or narcs." Christy raised her hands in supplication. "It was either talk to her or lose her as a contact."

"And you didn't see fit to share this with the homicide team?" Brandt sneered.

"I told Razulo."

Hillard sighed in exasperation. "Get Razulo in here ASAP," he ordered Brandt.

The sheriff excused himself for paperwork leaving the captain, the sergeant, and Christy alone in the briefing room.

"We're going to need you to write everything you remember, time and dates, in a report," Hillard said.

"Can she do it on the Coronita Substation computer?" Traynor asked. He was anxious to get Christy back on his home turf and away from headquarter politics.

"No, she needs to stay here."

Christy wondered if she'd ever be allowed back to the substation. Maybe they wanted to keep a closer eye on her by putting her in Records. That would mean moving back to Kearny.

"What about my car?" she asked.

Hillard looked at Traynor.

"Totaled," the sergeant replied gently.

Inwardly, she groaned. Okay, she was glad she survived but losing the Saturn was like losing a limb.

Brandt came back with Razulo dogging his footsteps. He withered under the captain's stare. They listened as he relayed his side of the story, even admitting the attempt to take the incriminating answering machine tape.

Christy was hustled out of the room before the real

reaming started. She could hear the profanity spill all the way down the hallway. Her own side of the story was taken down by a female sergeant, someone not involved with the case. Any disapproval from the woman was not discernible. Just the facts, ma'am.

When Christy got through it was nearly dark out. Sergeant Traynor hadn't deserted her and was waiting in the break room to take her home. He had a cold Dr Pepper waiting.

On the ride back to Coronita, Traynor said, "I asked the sheriff to give you a leave of absence. It's the least they can do for what they put you through up there."

Christy wanted to object but she agreed with her sergeant. Not only had she been forced to work at the beck and call of homicide, she'd worked overtime without compensation, been forced to live with a forest ranger, was nearly killed, demolished her car, and possibly ruined her relationship with Rodrigo. Yeah, she deserved a break.

"How long will I be off?"

Traynor looked over at her. "Take as much time as you need. But, there's a catch. You have to see the department shrink."

When Traynor dropped her off at the house, Christy found a welcoming committee waiting.

Lennie helped her out of the car, calling out to Traynor, "We'll take it from here."

Trace was standing on the porch, nursing a beer. Trina held a wriggling Shamus in her arms. Her landlady, Mrs. Alcorn, held a tray of chocolate chip cookies, and the upstairs tenant, Jonathan Maciel, tipped his beret before going back upstairs to his attic apartment. It wasn't a Norman Rockwell scenario, but it was home.

Was it a little over a week that she'd been gone? Christy looked at the familiarity of the apartment, amazed that everything was the same. The only thing that had changed in the interim was herself.

While Trina hustled into the kitchen, frying up tortillas for tacos, Christy slumped on the couch.

"Buck up, kiddo," Trace said as he squeezed in beside her. "You're home, you're safe, and surrounded by friends."

"I got a woman killed," Christy said softly. "She was helping us and she lost her life."

A look passed between Trace and Lennie.

"No, Patricia didn't die," Lennie said.

"What?" Surprise, relief, disbelief resounded in Christy's reaction.

"That's the good news." Lennie reached over and took Christy's arm. "She took a bullet in her spine. She's paralyzed from the waist down."

Guilt overwhelmed Christy. This time, there were no words.

"Tell her the rest, Lennie," Trace urged.

Lennie cleared her throat. "After she gets out of the hospital, she'll live in my house with Trace. We'll get her into physical therapy and hire a full-time nurse, the whole works. She deserves it for a lot of reasons. She'll be taken care of for the rest of her life."

Lennie, never short on generosity, could afford the burden helped by a healthy inheritance of Mt. Rainer Coffee stock. Christy nodded, understanding that it was a gesture to right some major wrongs done to the woman. It was also an attempt to alleviate Christy's guilt for putting Patricia in harm's way.

Tacos, cookies, Tylenol, and bed. Shamus brought a toy mouse to her and snuggled under the covers to knead her chest. Even safe in familiar surroundings, finally in the arms of friends, Christy only felt loss.

There was a lot of damage control to do before things would be close to normal again. She didn't want to think about it, she only wanted to sleep now and begin repairs in the morning.

Starting with her relationship with Rod.

About the Author

Sunny Frazier trained as a journalist and wrote for a city newspaper, military, and law enforcement publications. After working 17 years with the Fresno Sheriff's Department, 11 spent as a Girl Friday with an undercover narcotics team, it dawned on her that mystery writing was her real calling. Both *Fools Rush In* and *Where Angels Fear* are based on actual cases with a bit of astrology, a habit Frazier has developed over the past 42 years.